e for *The Field:*

"Readers will appreciate the fast-paced, compelling drama. A good choice for people who hope there's more to space than space."

—*Kirkus Reviews*

"Tracy Richardson is a worthy heir to Madeleine L'Engle. Richardson's characters intellectually travel beyond ordinary consciousness to delve into concepts of dark energy, collective [un]consciousness and universal energy fields."

—Rita Kohn, *NUVO Newsweekly*

"*The Field* is a brilliant blend of soccer, science and fiction. True-to-life characters, contemporary environmental issues, and engaging metaphysical principles skirt the edges of science fiction and magical realism in this modern coming-of-age novel."

—Laurie Gray, award-winning author of
Maybe I Will and *Summer Sanctuary*

"*The Field* plunges the reader into the realistic world of high school soccer and the mystical world of the Universal Energy Field—an intriguing combination."

—Judith L. Roth, author of *Serendipity and Me*

THE FIELD

THE FIELD

TRACY RICHARDSON

BROWN BOOKS
PUBLISHING GROUP

The Field

Brown Books Publishing Group
16250 Knoll Trail Drive, Suite 205
Dallas, Texas 75248
www.BrownBooks.com
(972) 381-0009

A New Era in Publishing®

Publisher's Cataloging-In-Publication Data

Names: Richardson, Tracy, author.
Title: The field / Tracy Richardson.
Description: Dallas, Texas : Brown Books Publishing Group, [2019]
Identifiers: ISBN 9781612543017
Subjects: LCSH: Extrasensory perception--Fiction. | College
    students--Psychology--Fiction. | Soccer players--
    Psychology--Fiction. | LCGFT: Paranormal fiction.
Classification: LCC PS3618.I3454 F54 2019 | DDC 813/.6--dc23

ISBN 978-1-61254-301-7
LCCN 2018957195

Printed in the United States
10 9 8 7 6 5 4 3 2 1

For more information or to contact the author,
please go to TracyRichardsonAuthor.com.

For my children, Alex and Katie, and all of their friends who hung out at our house and provided endless inspiration for my characters. Of course, the names have been changed to protect the innocent. Reid, you know who you are.

Also to the memory of Brett Finbloom, who left us too young. His spirit lives on.

"What we call empty space contains an immense background of energy. This vast sea of energy may play a key part in the understanding of the cosmos as a whole. Space, which has so much energy, is full rather than empty. What we perceive through the senses as empty space is actually the plenum, which is the ground for the existence of everything, including ourselves."

—David Bohm, physicist

1

A CAR HORN sounds outside. I grab my gym bag and water bottle off the kitchen chair.

"Bye, Mom. Will's here."

"Bye, Eric. Good luck!" Her disembodied voice floats down the stairs.

On the way out the side door, I pick up my soccer ball and dribble it with my feet down the driveway to Will's waiting Taurus. No small feat in flip-flops. The car's windows are down and the stereo is up—loud. The AC doesn't work, but we would still have the windows down to show off our good taste in music. I lob the ball through the back window, toss my gear in behind it and climb into the front. "The new system's totally tight," I say as I fasten my seatbelt.

"It's cool. Kind of makes up for driving a 'mom-mobile'." Will grins as he backs down the driveway.

"What do you mean? You've got your own wheels and it's a sedan. I have to drive the real 'mom-mobile'—the minivan. So, you ready for tonight?" I ask as I beat on the dashboard in time to the music.

"Yeah, two-a-day practices are brutal in ninety degree heat. I'm glad they're picking the teams tonight. What do you think our chances are?" Will glances over at me.

"Pretty good for Varsity. You're definitely the best defender and I don't think the other keepers are any better than me. We've been playing together so long, they can't break up our defensive unit," I say and give him a friendly punch on the shoulder. I do feel confident about our chances, but still. It's nerve-wracking to have three days of killer tryouts and not know for sure if you're on the team.

"I hate when they're calling out the names. Makes me sick to my stomach until my name's called." Will pushes his straight blond hair back from where it hangs over his eyes as he pulls into a parking spot at the field. "Well, good luck."

We walk over to the field trying to look calm and confident, and sit down to put on our cleats and shin guards before joining the rest of the guys for warm-ups. The coaches have been running us all week and tonight is no different. Even after running all summer to stay in shape, I was still gasping and sweating after the first day of tryouts. But I was in better shape than most of the guys—at least I didn't throw up. It's one way the coaches use to weed out players.

After doing a few wind sprints and running drills, they split everyone up into teams—freshmen, JV, and varsity. Will and I are both in the varsity group—*so far so good*. We all get one last opportunity to show our stuff before the cuts are made. I'm with the goalkeepers who are all grouped together and will be subbed in so we each get a chance to play.

As a group, the keepers are bigger than the field players. Taller and bulkier. At six foot two, I'm one of the taller ones. Tall and lean, though. More rangy than bulky. The field players need to be strong and fast and have incredible endurance to last the whole game. A keeper needs to be quick and explosive to move the instant a ball is shot, tall and strong to cover the whole goal and stop rocket shots, and fearless enough to dive into the air or at an opponent's moving feet without hesitation. I move away from the other keepers to begin focusing my thoughts. I always get a rush of adrenaline before a game or scrimmage and I want to channel it into performance instead of letting it turn into nervousness. I put on my gloves, fastening the Velcro at each wrist, and turn to watch the game.

Will is coming off the field when I get subbed in. We bump fists as he jogs past. He's jacked up and loose—he played great. "Nothing goes in, big guy!" he says. I just nod.

I position myself in the goal. I touch the left side of the goal, then walk to the right side, touch it, and then move to the center and touch the crossbar to orient myself. It's my ritual. I crouch in the center with my knees bent and arms in position to catch a ball. I feel confident, strong—ready. The coach starts the play.

The other team immediately takes control of the ball, and the play moves onto my side of the field. *Good. More action for me.*

The opposing team's striker sends the ball out to his right, and his midfielder runs onto it. I move to that side of the goal, and my left back covers the front. Our defender is all over the midfielder. I see that the opposing striker has moved into position in front of the goal to take a pass from the midfielder.

"Watch for the cross!" I yell. I've got the near post of the goal covered, coiled and ready to spring, and I want my center back to cover the forward.

The midfielder beats my defender and sends a pass through to his forward in front of the goal. I see it coming and leap out to punch the ball clear of the goal before the forward can head it in. My fist connects with the ball with a satisfying *thwack!* My center back takes the ball and sends it in a long arc to the other end of the field.

Yes! Adrenaline is surging through me and I'm pumped from stopping the cross. Now the play is on the other end of the field. I watch, staying focused on the action.

The other keeper makes a save and quickly punts the ball down the field before my defenders have moved back. The opposing forward runs onto the ball. He takes off, sprinting toward the goal, and beats my defender.

It's a breakaway! My heart is pounding. *It's just me and him.* The forward is approaching fast. *Should I come out to meet him and dive at his feet or stay big and block the shot?* It's a split-second decision. Make the wrong choice and it's a goal. *Wait!* A thought flashes into my consciousness. I *know* where the shot will be. *Left side—DIVE!* I'm off my feet almost before the forward's foot connects for the shot. I feel myself flying through the air, arms reaching. The ball is rocketing toward me. The ball strikes my palms and I push it wide, deflecting it outside of the goal, and then I crash to the ground.

I jump up quickly in case the ball is still in play. My team has control of the ball and is moving it down the field. Squinting into the sun, I watch the play. Adrenaline is coursing through my veins. *Total rush!*

When I get subbed out, I scan the sidelines for Will and jog over to him so we can rehash the play.

Will smacks me on the back. "You stuffed him!" Will's hair is dark with sweat, his face glistening and gritty. "How do you do that? I swear you were off the ground before he took the shot."

I wipe my face on my shirt and take a long drink from my water bottle before answering. "I don't know. Just reflexes, I guess." I don't want to make too big a deal about it with Will, but sometimes I just get a feeling of *knowing*. It just flashes into my head. Maybe it's from years of playing, but when it happens it feels different than reacting on instinct without thinking. It's like knowing without thinking.

"I bet it gets you a spot on varsity for sure. Maybe even starting."

"Yeah, well you were like a brick wall out there. Nothing got past you. Your keeper didn't have any saves to make."

"Thanks. Glad you noticed that you're not the only star out there."

"Whatever." I've been friends with Will forever and I know he's got my back, but there's always been a competitive side to our friendship. I'm thinking, *Right, how many saves did you make?* but I keep my mouth shut and turn my attention to the play on the field.

After all the players have had a chance to play and the scrimmage is over, the coaches have us run two cool-down laps around the field and then gather by the trainers' station to stretch. *This is it.* When they select the teams. But first the coaches go through this long speech about how everyone is a winner and good sportsmanship and how difficult it was for them to decide.

"We're hot, we're tired, and we stink," I say to the guys sitting next to me. "Just call out the names already." This elicits a rumble of laughter around me.

"OK, enough with the comments, Horton," Coach Swenson says. I shrug. "Let's get to it. Here are the teams. Freshmen first. When I call out your name, move over across the field to where Coach Vince is standing." He gestures to his right. He begins calling off the names for the freshman team and then the JV team. Each player jumps up when his name's called, relief on his face. Will and I wait through the JV names—we're not called. Now it's just the players who made varsity and those who didn't make it at all waiting on the grass. I have to believe that I made varsity, but there's still that small fear that I didn't make the cut.

"OK. Now for varsity," Coach Swenson calls out. "Ashmore, S., Asplunth, W." Will jumps up and I give him a high five. My heart is pounding. I'm waiting for the *H*s. "Bartlett, B., Cohen, A." My breathing is shallow, like I'm holding my breath. "Franklin, M., Gordon, S., Horton, E." It feels like my heart actually stops for an instant. Horton! Varsity! I made varsity! I jump up and jog over to the group surrounding Coach Vince.

"Eric, all right!" They clap me on the back. "Congratulations," says Coach Vince and shakes my hand. Will grabs my shoulders. "Hey, man! We're on varsity!"

"I know," I say stupidly. I actually feel a little wobbly in the knees, the relief is so great. "Varsity. I know." I lay down spread-eagled on the grass and savor the moment. The coolness of the grass feels wonderful. *Yes! Varsity!* But then I hear the coach call out 'Morgan, B.'—*Brett Morgan*—the second-string varsity keeper from last year who's a senior this year. My euphoria dims. I'll have to beat him out to get the starting spot. What good is it to be on varsity if I sit on the bench?

2

I STRUGGLE TO get my locker open for the third time. Why do I always get the crappy lockers? OK, just turn the dial to the last number and quickly lift the handle. It catches and I open the locker door. *Finally.* I start loading books from my backpack into the empty space. Kids are swarming through the hallway, rushing around before the first bell rings.

"Good day, young scholar." My friend Cole leans up against the locker next to mine.

I smile to myself. "Hey." I can see his feet from my bent-over vantage point. "Nice toe socks." He's wearing rainbow-striped toe socks with flip-flops. As I stand up, I see that his skinny legs are sticking out of blue jean cut-offs. "And shorts. Did I miss the text? Is the first day of school '80s day?"

"You like? I joined the Gay-Straight Alliance and I'm showing solidarity with the rainbow socks. The '80s look is just a bonus."

"It's definitely in line with your anti-establishment position." A group of girls passes us and one calls out, "Hey, Eric. Hey, Cole—cute socks!" They all laugh.

"The unexpected bonus is the chick magnet factor. Who knew?" Cole smiles his lopsided grin.

"Yeah, who knew? But don't they all think you're gay? That kind of cuts down on the hookup potential."

"Well, there is that to consider." Cole is unabashed. I shake my head.

"What's your schedule this year? Did you drop AP Environmental Science?" Even though he tries to hide it with lack of ambition, Cole is pretty smart.

"No, my parents applied the pressure/guilt trip that I need an advanced placement class to get into college, and I caved. At least it's a cool class, and Mr. Ogle isn't bad, from what I hear."

"Yeah, it's supposed to be a fantastic class. Man, it's freezing in here. They've got the air cranked full blast." I'm shivering in my shorts and T-shirt. I grab my hoodie out of my backpack, pull it on and shake out my hair.

"Do you find your luxurious wavy brown locks to be a chick magnet? Girls do seem to like the shaggy soccer player look." The fluorescent lights are reflecting off of Cole's glasses and I can't tell from his face if he's serious or not.

I give him a look. "If you say so." Over Cole's shoulder I see Will approaching through the throng of students. The three of us have been friends since elementary school. He claps a hand on Cole's shoulder.

"Starting the year off on the right foot, Cole?" His gaze is on the toe socks. "Are you guys ready for AP Enviro?" Will is tanned and rock solid from spending the summer working construction and playing soccer. I know I don't look too bad myself from being outside so much and working out. I'd like to think that's a better way to attract girls than wearing toe socks. The first bell rings.

"Yup. Ready." I slam my locker shut with my shoulder. "Let's go."

We make our way through the sea of humanity that is the student body of Monroe High School. As juniors we've been through the drill before, but it's still incredible how many kids are here. One thousand per grade. Our lockers are in the junior hallway, so we see a lot of kids we know. But still. How many can you know out of one thousand people?

I follow Will into the classroom and glance around the room as the second bell rings. Most people are talking or taking out their notebooks. A dark-haired girl is sitting in the front row by the door. She looks up as we walk in. My gaze brushes hers, and my breath catches in my throat. A sudden zing runs through me, almost like a jolt of recognition. I must've stopped in my tracks, because Cole crashes into me from behind and I stumble, breaking the eye contact.

"Gentlemen, please take your seats," says Mr. Ogle.

We grab three seats in the back, and I check out the girl from there. I've never seen her before. I would've remembered. Her straight dark hair falls below her shoulders, and she is sitting sideways in her chair, facing the front, so I can see her profile. She's pretty in an unconventional way. Not Barbie doll pretty; more dramatic, with her dark hair and pale skin. I kick Cole's foot across the aisle.

"Who's that girl?" I whisper.

He shrugs. "Wouldn't you like to know?"

"Yeah. Do you know her?"

"Negative."

Mr. Ogle starts going through the usual first day of school routine, handing out the class 'rules' and syllabus with the website info.

"Welcome to Advanced Placement Environmental Science, where we explore all aspects of environmental science, including

9

chemical, physical, and biological. This year we'll be focusing a lot of attention on traditional and alternative energy sources and how their usage affects the environment. We have field trips scheduled to the Benton County Wind Farm and the Eagle River Coal Gasification Plant." *Cool. Field trips are always a good thing.* Will is sitting in the seat in front of me and I tap him on the back of the head with my pen. His dad works at the Coal Gasification Plant. He reaches behind his head and tries to grab my hand.

"And I am pleased to tell you that we will have a very prestigious guest lecturer visit us this year. Dr. Auberge is a distinguished nuclear energy physicist visiting from the world renowned Overet Lab in France who is studying cutting-edge areas of alternative energy sources. He's spending two years at the university and has agreed to come and teach a few of our classes, and," Mr. Ogle pauses for effect and glances around the room to make sure he has everyone's attention, "he is offering an internship in his lab, starting second semester, to one of the students in this class."

There is a general murmuring in the room as everyone digests this bit of information. It's usually a pretty competitive group in the AP classes, so there's sure to be some interest. "Also, we have a new student in the class who happens to be Dr. Auberge's daughter. Please welcome Renee Auberge." He extends his hand toward the dark-haired girl by the classroom door. *Renee.* She inclines her head and smiles.

"Vous-êtes Française, mademoiselle Auberge?" Cole asks. *Geez.*

"Oui," she answers in a clear, lilting voice—at least to my ears.

"Bienvenue à Monroe High," says Cole, and he stands up and actually *bows.*

"*Merci.* Thank you," she answers. It looks like she's trying not to laugh. She's looking at Cole, but could she also be looking at me? I nod and smile at her and she nods back. Will turns around slightly in his seat and gives me a lecherous look. *Great.* I hope that doesn't mean that she's caught his interest too. Maybe he's thinking about the internship. I raise my eyebrows at him and shrug.

"Thank you, Mr. Rosenberg, for acting as our welcoming committee," Mr. Ogle says. Cole makes a flourish in the air with his hand and inclines his head slightly before sitting down. "OK, now we have a lot to cover this year, so let's get started. First semester we'll focus on human energy consumption and its effects on the environment. We'll look at the current practice of extracting and burning fossil fuels and compare that to alternative sources such as solar, wind, nuclear and so-called clean coal." I see Will bristle at Mr. Ogle's remark. "Hence the field trips."

I take out my binder and start taking notes. The lecture is actually pretty interesting, and I've been looking forward to this class. Mr. Ogle is one of the cooler teachers, but he's still kind of goofy in his corduroys and button down shirt—like he's trying to dress like one of the hipster crowd instead of being stuck in the same '80s time warp as Cole.

Forty-five minutes later the bell rings, and everyone slams shut their notebooks and starts gathering up their stuff. I glance toward the door at Renee. She's putting her books into her book bag. I grab my backpack, slide out of my chair, and make my way over to her before I lose my nerve. I stop in front of her desk and she looks up at me.

"Uh, hi, um, I'm Eric Horton. And, ah, I can't say it in French like Cole, but welcome to Monroe." She looks at me with a slight smile like she's waiting for me to say something else. My mind goes completely blank for a moment. Then I quickly say, "I could show you around school, ah, if you want, sometime. It's a pretty big place." *When—hopefully that didn't come off as completely stupid.*

"Thank you." She smiles, and it lights up her face and crinkles the corners of her green eyes. "I did get a tour and I have a map, but I could use some directions in finding my next class," she says in perfect, slightly accented English.

"Sure. Show me the map. What room is your next class in?"

"Uh, let me see." She stands up, propping her book bag on the desk, and reaches into its outside pocket with long, slim fingers to retrieve her schedule and a map of the school. "It's comparative lit in A238. What section are we in now?"

"We're in C section—science and math—second floor. You'll need to go back over to the rotunda and then into the English department in section A. Here, let me show you." I reach for the map and my fingers brush hers. Her skin is smooth and I feel that jolt to my gut again. I glance up at Renee, and her eyes are wide with surprise. *Does she feel it too?* I quickly take the map, unfold it, and smooth it out on her desk. "Just follow this hallway to section C's center hallway and then over to the rotunda down this hallway and into section A. Don't worry, you'll get used to it. Each section is like a spoke coming out from the rotunda and they're all the same."

"If you say so," she says with a laugh. "Well, thank you again, Eric Horton. I'm pretty sure I can find my way now."

"No problem. See you in class tomorrow." I hand her back the map, careful not to brush her fingers this time, and smile what I hope is a confident, friendly smile.

"Bye." She slings her book bag over her shoulder and enters the crowded hallway.

I pick up my own backpack from where I dropped it on the floor. *Maybe I should have offered to take her to her class.* Then I feel a hand on my shoulder and Will's voice in my ear. "She's *hot!*"

"Yeah, but I got to her first." I say it lightly, but I really don't like hearing him talk about her like that. No matter how hot she is.

Will backs away and holds up his hands in mock surrender. "I see how it is. Anyway, I already have a girlfriend. She's all yours, big guy."

"It's not like that," I say, annoyed. Will raises his eyebrow questioningly. "I mean, I just said hello to her."

"Whatever," he says. "Gotta get to US History. What lunch do you have? I've got B lunch."

"Me, too. I'll catch up to you then."

"Later."

As I jostle through the crowd in the hallway on the way to my Calculus class, I wonder about my reaction to Will and the weird feeling I got around Renee. I mean, I barely know her, but . . . what? There was something there between us. At least for me. And I just didn't like Will saying that about her. I shake my head to clear my thoughts and head toward the central stairwell.

ACROSS THE CAFETERIA I see a table with some of my friends from soccer. I make my way over to them with my tray and take a seat.

"Eric, hey!" Paul says and gives me a five-star right between my shoulder blades. *Uoof*—the air is forced out of my lungs. Thankfully, I hadn't started eating yet. I return the greeting by punching him in the arm—hard.

"Yow! You been working out?" He feels my biceps. "Coach Swenson says we've got a great team this year." He's talking through a mouthful of garlic toast. "We're stoked to have you on varsity." Paul's a senior and team captain. "When do you find out if you're starting?"

I swallow a mouthful of spaghetti before responding, "I don't think we'll know until the first game." I'd thought about it all weekend. I *am* going to beat out the other keeper. My dad's real big on visualizing the outcome that you want, and I've read some sports psychology stuff about it, so I've been imagining myself making great saves in practice and walking out on the field to start in the first game. I'm not sure how effective it really is, but what the hell? Our first game is a home game on Friday night. Will and Cole join the table and sit across from me.

"So, what do you think about AP Enviro? That internship sounds interesting. And Renee is definitely interesting," Will says.

"Yeah, it could be cool. It would definitely look good on a college application." I ignore his comment about Renee. I know he's baiting me.

"Well, I have something interesting to share," says Cole. "I've already paid a visit to the dean's office." He looks almost proud of himself.

"What?! We're not even through the first day of school. What happened?" asks Will.

"During the Pledge of Allegiance in third period home room, I exercised my right not to stand and say the pledge. Mr. Smitson insisted that I do so and when I respectfully refused, he sent me to the dean's office."

"Oh, man! On the first day," exclaims Will.

"He must not know that your mom's a civil rights attorney," I say, laughing.

"Apparently not."

"Why didn't you just stand and say the damn pledge?" asks Paul.

"It's my right not to, as an American citizen, granted by the Constitution."

"That doesn't make any sense. You object to the pledge using the rights granted to you by the Constitution?" Paul says.

"It's 'the man' that I object to, the establishment, the right wing government. Not the Constitution."

"OK, whatever, let's not get off on that tangent. So what did the dean do?" I ask.

"Well, on the way down to the office, I called my mom to alert her to the situation. When I arrived at the dean's office and explained my position, she laughed and told me to go easy on Mr. Smitson. She sent me back to class with a note. On the way back I called my mom to tell her the situation was handled."

"Wow. This would only happen to you, Cole." I lean back in my chair and balance it on two legs while holding on to the edge of the table. "You just can't go with the flow."

The bell rings. "Man, they only give us like ten minutes to eat," Paul says and shovels the last few bites of spaghetti into his mouth.

"Paul, that is just gross. Would you at least close your mouth?" says Will. He pushes back his chair and picks up his tray. "See you guys at practice."

"*Adios*," I reply. I walk over and deposit my tray on the conveyer belt piled high with trays and trash slowly disappearing through a flapped window into the kitchen. Our first team practice is after school today. The hard part about competing with the other keepers for the starting spot is that most of the time we all train together, separate from the field players, since our position is so specialized. *I'll have to strike the right balance of competitiveness and cooperation to make the cut,* I think as I make my way to my afternoon classes.

3

My mom is in the kitchen when I get home from practice. I toss my backpack on the kitchen table, open the fridge, and take out a gallon of milk.

"How was your day?" She asks me the same thing every day.

"Good." I pour myself a glass of milk and rip open a package of Oreos from the pantry.

"Anything interesting happen? And don't eat too many of those; dinner's in about half an hour." This question must be from one of her parenting books, designed to elicit conversation, since she uses it a lot.

"Well, Cole wore rainbow-striped toe socks and got sent to the dean's office," I reply, pulling a stool out from under the counter at the island and sitting down.

"For wearing toe socks?" She's rinsing green beans in a bowl at the sink and turns to look at me incredulously.

"No, for refusing to stand and recite the Pledge of Allegiance."

"Oh, please. Don't they have more serious discipline problems than that? Really." My mom's actually not that bad, just kind of lame. She and my dad are pretty easy to talk to about stuff—

when I want to talk, that is. They don't freak out too much when you bring things up.

"Yeah, the dean just laughed about it and sent him back to class." The back door to the garage opens and my dad walks in. He puts his keys and wallet in one of the cubbyholes over the desk and his briefcase on the floor, then comes over and puts a hand on my shoulder.

"Hey! How was the first day back at school and the first day of practice?" He sits down on the stool next to me and takes a cookie.

"Not you, too! No more cookies, please! Dinner'll be ready soon," Mom exclaims as she fills a pot with water and dumps the beans into it.

We ignore her and keep eating. "It was OK. AP Environmental Science seems pretty good. Lots of field trips."

"Where to?"

"The Benton County Wind Farm and the Coal Gasification Plant. Maybe some others."

"The wind farm is pretty amazing. I drove past it last spring on my way to one of our satellite campuses. All of a sudden in the middle of the cornfields, these giant turbines appear. There must be hundreds of them. I've read that it's going to be the biggest wind farm east of the Mississippi when it's completed. Not what you'd expect from the coal belt. Makes you proud to be from Indiana." He puts his hand over his heart in an exaggerated gesture of pride.

"I guess so." I'm about to tell them about the internship when my dad asks where Marcie and Drew are.

"Drew's down the street with some friends and Marcie should be dropped off from cross country practice any minute now," my mom answers. Marcie is my fourteen-year-old sister—she's a freshman this year, and Drew is in third grade.

"All right, then. Is there time for me to go for a run before dinner?" Dad asks.

"Sure, if you swing by the Reeds' on the way back to get Drew."

"Consider it done." He starts getting up from the island.

I quickly say, "Have you heard anything about an important physics professor visiting at the university from the Overet Lab in France? He's going to teach a couple of AP Enviro classes." I pause. "And he's offering an internship in his lab for second semester."

"Wow, really?" My dad sits back down. "So, you're interested? I haven't heard about him, but I wouldn't in the English department. What about you, Jill?"

"I might have heard something, but archeologists don't mingle too much with the physics department, either." I have their full attention now. My mom's leaning on the island, dish towel in hand. As professors at the university, my parents are *really* big on education, so I figured they would be all over this.

"He's a nuclear physicist studying alternative energy sources. The internship could be cool."

"So, do you want us to look into it for you or anything?" my dad asks, a little too casually. "We could call some of our colleagues to put in a good word." My parents are always so helpful. It can be annoying.

"No, definitely not. I don't even know anything about it or how he will choose the intern."

"OK. Well, let us know how it goes."

As I'm gathering my gear to take upstairs and then get in the shower, Marcie comes in noisily from the side door and dumps her bags—she has at least four, and I have no idea what she has in all of them—all over the floor by the door.

"Hey!" my mom says. "How was your first day of high school?"

"It was great! Sara is in my English class and I have A lunch with a lot of my friends." She takes my stool at the island and I decide I'd better get upstairs quick to shower before she gets in and uses all the hot water.

AFTER DINNER I go up to my room to get started on my homework. Even though it's just the first day of school, my teachers didn't hold back on assignments. It's mostly reading, so I stack the pillows on my bed against the headboard and get my iPhone so I can listen to music while I start the novel we're reading for English. It's *A Farewell to Arms* by Hemingway, which is supposed to be pretty good, so I figure it's a good place to start. Ralph, the mutt we got from the pound last year, jumps on the bed and makes a nest in the comforter by my feet. He circles around several times and then lies down with a sigh, nose to tail.

My room's not too bad. I've got a full-sized bed and matching dresser that was once my grandparents', and even though my mom wanted to 'decorate,' I held out and only let her paint the walls. It's kind of a mess, but I like it that way. Actually, I just don't put away my clothes, so they're all over the floor, and fortunately my parents aren't too crazy about making me keep my room clean.

I settle in and start reading. After a while I feel myself getting sleepy. I have to keep re-reading the same words over again and my eyes are drooping. Even the tunes aren't enough to keep me awake. A full day of school and then two hours of practice really take it out of you. Then two or three hours of homework on top of that? It's nuts, really, what they expect us to do.

I close the book and lay my head back on the pillows. I'm thinking I'll just close my eyes and rest for a few minutes and then start back in. That feeling you get of floating away just before you fall asleep starts to come over me, and I must doze off for a while. The explosion rocks me from my sleep.

Flashes of orange, black, and yellow light explode in my head along with a tremendous crashing noise. I jerk abruptly awake and cry out. Ralph is so startled he jumps up and barks at me. At first, I think something must have happened outside or downstairs, because my room looks the same as always. But then I realize it was some sort of awful dream. A nightmare. I sit on the edge of my bed with my feet hanging over the side and hold my head in my hands. I'm so shook up that I'm actually trembling. I take a deep breath and blow it out. *What the hell?* I don't usually have nightmares. I know I must dream, but they never stay with me long in the morning. This was really vivid. Scary. It felt like I could actually hear the explosion.

Studying isn't going to happen until I can get my heart to stop pounding, and I figure I could do with a little fresh air and change of scenery. "You wanna go for a walk?" I say to Ralph. He definitely knows that word because he immediately jumps down from the bed and starts wagging his tail. He races ahead of me down the stairs, looking back to see if I'm coming for the promised walk. In the kitchen, Drew is sitting at the table doing his homework with my parents nearby in the family room, ready to offer their help. Like I said, they are very helpful. Not that it's a bad thing, I'm just saying. After a certain point, you don't want their help all the time anymore.

"I'm going to take Ralph on a walk around the block."

"Take Speck with you, too." My dad calls from the couch.

"All right. Speck, do you want to go for a walk?" Speck leaps down from her spot on the arm of my mom's chair and scampers over to me, her whole body wagging with excitement. She's our cairn terrier, and she wouldn't be my first choice for a walk because she has to stop and sniff everything, but how can I deny her such joy? Their leashes are hanging on a hook by the back door. Ralph sits stock still waiting for me to snap it to his collar, as if to say, "I'm a good dog, look how good I'm being for my walk." At least that's what I imagine he's thinking. Speck, on the other hand, can't keep still and wiggles all over the place in anticipation, making it hard for me to clip on her leash.

I open the back door and they scramble down the steps, pulling me along. Night comes late in August, and the sun is just now setting. It's a fantastic sunset with streaks of purple, blue, pink, and orange in the western sky over the trees and the rooftops. Large, dusky blue clouds on the horizon almost look like low hills in the distance. The eastern sky is dark with a few stars already winking.

We walk down the driveway with Ralph pulling on his leash to go forward and Speck sniffing around in the bushes. As we walk into the pool of light under the street lamp at the end of the driveway, it abruptly blinks out. It's not that big a deal in and of itself, but it happens to me a lot. Enough so that I've started to become aware of overhead lights going on or off when I pass beneath them. It mostly happens with street lamps and lights in parking lots and garages. This particular light does it a lot, but it doesn't always do it, which makes it even weirder. It's kind of unpredictable, so that I'll forget about it for weeks and even months, and then *blink* it happens again.

I take the dogs to the end of the block and then turn around and come back. When we pass under the light at the end of the driveway, it abruptly comes back on, startling me, its glow illuminating the night and creating elongated, giant shadows of me and the dogs on the pavement.

4

IT'S A FEW minutes after the first bell, and I want to get to class at just the right time. I pause at the door and work up my courage. *It's no big deal, I'm just going to sit next to her.* I'm hoping she's already sitting at the seat by the door where she's been the last two days. If it's close to the second bell, then I can just grab the seat behind her like I'm in a hurry. When I step through the doorway, I avoid looking toward the back of the classroom where Will and Cole and I usually sit, so I don't have to make eye contact with them. That would be really distracting. Renee is in her seat by the door. Thankfully, the seat behind her is empty, and I slide into it just as the second bell rings. *Perfect.* As I pass by her, I get a hint of lemon and I catch her eye. "Hey," I say.

"Hi, Eric." She smiles at me, crinkling her green eyes. My nervousness disappears, and I smile back.

I glance up at the front of the classroom as I pull my books out. Mr. Ogle is there, and so is another dark-haired man taking papers and a flash drive out of his briefcase.

"All right, everyone, time to pay attention," Mr. Ogle begins. "As you recall, I told you that we would be honored this year to have the distinguished Dr. Auberge from the Overet Nuclear

Institute teach some of our classes on alternative energy sources. He is here today, so please give him your undivided attention."

Renee's father. Somehow that seems more important to me than his being a prominent physicist.

"Good morning. I am pleased to be here with you today. It's exciting for me to talk with our next generation of scientists, as you will be on the forefront of making the new discoveries that will most likely change the world as we know it." He speaks with slightly accented English like Renee and has the same glossy dark hair. Physically, he's not very imposing—he's medium height and medium build—but he has an intensity about him that grabs my attention.

"For the first part of my lecture, I will talk with you about the work that I do at the Overet Nuclear Institute and France's Nuclear Energy Commission. Then I will touch upon the studies and experiments I will be conducting during the two years I am at the university on a research sabbatical. Please feel free to ask questions as we go along." He leans down to insert his flash drive into the laptop and pulls up his presentation. A picture of two large circular towers against a cloudless blue sky appears on the screen.

"France is a country with very few natural energy resources. No oil, no natural gas, and negligible amounts of very poor quality coal. In the early 1970s, during the Mid-East Energy Crisis, France made the decision to focus on nuclear energy in order to become energy independent. Now, over 76 percent of France's electricity is generated by nuclear plants and another 14 percent is produced by hydropower. Carbon dioxide emissions throughout the country are extremely low and have actually decreased over the last thirty years." Surprised, I look up from my notes. I knew that France used nuclear energy, but I didn't realize that they weren't dependent on the Middle East for oil. Dr. Auberge continues. "We achieved energy independence and reduced pollution using nuclear power. There is, however, still the issue of nuclear waste and, to a lesser extent, the danger of accidents and radiation to contend with. In light of the failure of Japan's nuclear plant after the earthquake and tsunami in 2010, nuclear accidents are a bigger concern to the public."

Sitting behind Renee, I can check her out unobtrusively while I look toward the front of the room. Her smooth, dark hair falls forward, obscuring her face as she leans over her desk taking notes, and she reaches up to push it behind her ear. The gesture makes the silver bracelets on her wrist clink together and slide down the pale skin of her arm. I don't know what makes people attracted to each other, but I know I'm definitely attracted to her.

"While the French people are comfortable living near nuclear reactors, that is not the case in other countries such as the United States, and no one wants the storage facilities for radioactive nuclear waste in their backyard. It is a problem that will need to be resolved if we are to continue to use nuclear energy." I keep taking notes as Dr. Auberge goes on with his lecture. Fortunately, it's pretty basic stuff, so I can keep up even as I'm distracted when Renee crosses her legs and later when she stretches her neck from side-to-side, making her hair swing across her back and her perfume waft past me.

"Now, to switch gears," Dr. Auberge says and turns off the presentation. "While I am here at the university, I will be researching a different and emerging area of study concerning the Universal Energy Field." I go over the words "Energy Field" that I just wrote in my notes to darken them and then circle them several times. The room is quiet. He has everyone's attention. "It is also called the 'Zero Point Field.' It is easiest to think of it in this manner. We know that the air around us is filled with energy waves or forces. Magnetic, sound, light, radio, television, microwave, radiation, et cetera. Most of these waves are outside the realm of human perception. However, we can measure them, and we know that animals can hear sounds that are imperceptible to the human ear, and we benefit from the action of these waves when we watch TV, use our cell phones, or microwave our dinner."

Dr. Auberge paces back and forth in front of the room, gesturing for emphasis. "Scientists theorize that there is enough energy in a cubic inch of space *anywhere in the universe* to power all of New York City for a year." He stops and looks around the room. Someone coughs and clears his throat.

"What we don't fully know yet is how to harness these powerful forces as an infinite energy source. That is the focus of my research and experiments for the next two years." Whoa. I sit back in my chair. This is like something from Star Trek. I try to imagine what it would mean if we could access limitless energy from the air around us. Dr. Auberge continues. "Think of the implications of a totally clean, infinitely renewable energy source. No more drilling for oil or natural gas or mining for coal. No more burning fossil fuels and the resulting air pollution. No need for nuclear power and radioactive waste." A boy on the other side of the room raises his hand. Dr. Auberge points to him. "Yes?"

"So, do you mean that right here in this room around us there is enough energy to power, like, the whole United States? "

"That is what we believe to be the case."

"Why haven't we heard more about it?"

"As I said, it is an emerging area of science. Not all scientists agree with these theories. Something this different from what we think we know is often hard for people to understand or accept. In fact, the idea of the Universal Energy Field has been around for over one hundred years and was first proposed by scientists such as Nikola Tesla, who invented the system of alternating current that all of our electricity runs on today, and Michael Faraday, who is credited with pioneering the motor. Even over two thousand years ago, Peredices referred to the cosmos as the 'plenum.' More recently, David Bohm, Ervin Laszlo, and Eric Heim risked their careers by postulating the existence of the Universal Energy Field in the face of opposition by their peers."

"How can there be energy in outer space? Isn't it a vacuum?" a girl with kinky brown hair in the front row—I think her name is Emily—asks.

"There is no atmosphere in space as there is here on earth, but it is not empty. Quantum mechanics has demonstrated that there is no such thing as a vacuum or nothingness. The universe is essentially a sea of energy. Scientists are calling it 'Dark Energy,' and while we don't know exactly what it is, Einstein predicted its existence when he postulated using a 'cosmological constant' to explain the expansion of the universe. This energy exists. The idea of accessing and harnessing Dark Energy seems like science fiction to some, but believe me, *it is very real.* We have to set aside what we think we know about the world around us and open our minds to new discoveries. Remember, we once thought the world was flat, and Galileo was thrown in jail for suggesting that the earth revolved around the sun." He pauses and sits down on the edge of Mr. Ogle's desk. "Just because you can't see it and you don't understand it, doesn't mean it isn't real."

That pretty much shuts people up. I look around to gauge everyone's reactions. There are some people with their arms crossed, looking skeptical, and one guy with his head down on his desk, probably asleep, but more than a few of the kids look really intrigued. I mean, it's pretty cool to have someone like Dr.

Auberge, who's on the cutting edge of science, talk to your class. Renee is sitting quietly in front of me looking straight ahead, so I can't see her face.

"I believe Mr. Ogle has told you that I will have an internship opportunity beginning next semester. Once I have determined the selection process, he will share that with you. I am also looking for subjects for some experiments I am conducting on remote viewing. We are interested in 'bonded pairs' such as husbands and wives or, in your case, boyfriends and girlfriends, close friends, teammates, and the like. People who have close relationships with one another. We pay a small stipend for each session. If you are interested in participating, you can fill out one of these questionnaires for my staff to evaluate whether you are suitable for the study, or stop by the lab to apply."

He pulls a sheaf of papers from his briefcase and sets them on the corner of the table at the front of the room. "Thank you for your attention this morning." He inclines his head slightly.

"OK, class, let's show Dr. Auberge our appreciation," says Mr. Ogle, as he begins clapping. The room erupts into applause. "Also, remember your reading assignment for tomorrow," he says loudly to be heard over the din as the bell rings. *Now's my chance.*

"Renee." I tap her on the shoulder, and she turns halfway around in her seat to face me. "Our first home soccer game is this Friday night. You might want to go." *You might want to go?* That sounded stupid and cocky.

"Are you asking me to go with you?" she asks, looking at me sideways.

"No, um, I'm on the team, but I, ah, thought that maybe after the game we could go out or something," I stammer. I hold my breath.

"Sure, I would like that. What position do you play?"

"I'm the goalkeeper." *Hopefully, the starting keeper.*

"In France we call it football."

"I think the US is the only place in the world that calls it soccer. Why don't you give me your number, and I'll text you about where we can meet after the game." She takes out a pen and rips a piece of paper from her notebook.

"Here's my number. I'll wait to hear from you." She gathers her books and stands up to leave. "See you later." She puts her hand on my arm briefly and then turns and leaves the classroom. I look at the paper. It says *Renee* and then her number in big, loopy script. Almost like calligraphy. *Yes!*

5

"Ooof." THE BALL Brett just drilled hits me right in the gut. I catch it and exaggerate holding it to my chest for a moment before dropping it to the side and getting ready for the next one. It's not just about making the save, but also about posturing. The coaches are watching. Brett's being particularly vicious with his shots. It's pretty obvious that we're competing for the starting spot. We're nice to each other off the field and all, but since it's just the two of us on varsity and the keepers from all three teams train together, it's cutthroat on the field. His next shot is high and to my right; I jump and stretch to reach it and tip the ball over the crossbar. "Switch!" calls out Coach Vince. I pump my fists down at my sides as I leave the goal—*shut out—no goals!*

The first hour of practice is conditioning and drills. We've already done our warm-up laps and stretches and then forty-five minutes of keeper drills. They're pretty brutal. Catching balls from standing, sitting and lying down, and every other combination. It makes for rock hard abs and a really sore body from getting pummeled by balls and repeatedly hitting the ground. I love it.

The coaches give us a break before we scrimmage, so I jog over to the water station, even though I'm pretty whipped from just saving twenty shots. Keeping up the image. The field players are already there and everyone is drinking a lot. Some of the guys are pouring water over their heads to cool down. August is probably the hottest part of the summer in Indiana and it's incredibly humid. On top of that, it hasn't really rained in about two weeks, so the ground is hard and cracked and the grass on the training field is dry and crispy. It's like diving on cement covered with sand paper. I walk over to Paul and Will.

"Dude, I really hate the Track of Death," Paul is saying. He's bent over with his hands on the ground stretching out his legs.

"Yeah, Coach Bobby is a sadist," Will replies. "I lose six pounds sweating every day during practice. Hey," he says to me, crumpling his paper cup and tossing it into the trash can.

"Is that the one where you sprint longer and longer intervals, and if you're last you have to jog around the field the whole time?" I ask.

"Yup. It's brutal. At least we get to scrimmage now—that's what it's all about."

They've been putting Will and me together for the scrimmages, which is what we want, and we're on the A squad, so hopefully that means they're going to start us both. Playing together over the years, Will and I have developed a kind of teamwork that goes beyond just executing plays and talking on the field. It's like we know each other so well we can anticipate what the other is going to do by the way we move our body or incline our head.

"OK, everybody, listen up!" Coach Vince yells. "Varsity is scrimmaging JV. A squad's in first." *This could be too easy.* I want to get as much action as possible. Will and I walk over to the field together. I orient myself in the goal and tighten the Velcro on my gloves. I'm facing west, which sucks because the sun is in my face. Will moves into position in defense. The coach blows the whistle and play begins. Varsity takes the ball and moves it to the other end of the field. I watch the action with my arm shielding my eyes from the sun. One of the JV players gets the ball and they move it down the field toward me. Now a JV forward and a varsity fullback are fighting for possession in the corner, giving the other players time to move into position in front of the goal.

The JV forward jukes around the fullback and passes to the middle. There's a crowd in front of the goal, which means there isn't a clear shot, but also means my view is obstructed and increases the possibility of deflections I can't anticipate. I'm moving in the goal, following the play and calling out instructions to my defense. I see a JV player get the ball—*he's going to shoot!* I get big—arms down and out to the side, fingers splayed, knees bent—he shoots—the ball ricochets off my arm into the crush in front of the goal. *Save!* My defenders need to clear it. *Where is Will?* I can't see the ball. One of my defenders is screening me. I move to get a clear look and then *whoosh*—I feel the ball whiz past me into the back of the goal. *Shit!* I kick the ball into the net. Then I punch the goalpost. Hard. Which hurts. A lot. Will is next to me. He puts his hand on my shoulder.

"Hey, shake it off, big guy. It's just one goal. Anyway, you were screened."

"You should've cleared it. Where were you?" I say angrily. I know I shouldn't blame Will or the defenders, but I hate being scored on. Especially now with the starting spot on the line. I'm also surprised that Will wasn't there to clear the ball. He's usually all over it. My 'unstoppable defensive unit' theory is blown to hell.

"Not cool, dude." Will gives me a hard look and stands with his hands on his hips. "Don't be a jerk. Show some leadership."

"Yeah, sorry. I'm just pissed. That was a crappy goal." I wipe my face on my sleeve and then clap my gloved hands together. "OK, come on guys!" I yell. "Put the pressure on!"

Will turns away. "That's what I'm talking about," he says over his shoulder. "But you're still a jerk." He's smiling, though, as he says it.

"Thanks. You, too!" I say and wave at him mockingly. Then I crouch down and do a couple squat jumps. *Focus. Next one is DENIED!*

The rest of the scrimmage goes pretty well. I make some good saves. Brett gets scored on once, too, but it was really bad. When the ball was shot, it caught him totally off guard. He didn't even move. He just stood there and watched it go by. It was totally savable. He did get in a couple good saves, though. It's hard to tell who the coaches will go with to start tomorrow night.

After practice, as we walk to the parking lot where his car is parked, Will asks, "What do you think about Dr. Auberge and that Energy Field stuff from AP Enviro?"

"I thought it was pretty cool, but a little out there. I mean, it's incredible to think about it, and as my little brother is always saying, 'anything's possible.'"

"Yeah, totally. I was thinking we might sign up for that study he's doing with pairs, since we're teammates. It might help with the internship, and we could make some money. Maybe get you in good with Renee's dad, too. You interested?" He stops to unlock his car with his key and gives me a sly look. The Taurus is so old, it doesn't have a remote opener.

"Sure, why not? But I don't think getting in good with Dr. Auberge will get me anywhere with Renee." I slide into the passenger seat and put my bag on the floor by my feet. "I asked her if she wanted to get together after the game tomorrow night." My turn to give the sly look.

"Whoa, dude! What'd she say?" Will slaps his leg and then puts the car in reverse.

"She said yes." I can't help smiling. *She said yes.*

WILL DROPS ME off in my driveway. I grab a drink from the fridge in the garage on my way into the house and drop my bag by the laundry machine. My soccer clothes need immediate attention. I'm supposed to be doing my own laundry, but I've discovered that if I leave my dirty clothes in the laundry room my mom will usually do it for me. Hope springs eternal. In the kitchen, my mom is talking on her cell phone and still wearing her work clothes. She's crashing around with the pots and pans, too. The total multi-tasker. I'm about to head upstairs to shower when she stops me. "I need you to pick up Drew from his soccer practice after you shower."

"Aww, come on, Mom. I need a break. I've been gone all day," I say, knowing it probably won't work, but it's worth a try.

"Well, I've been gone all day, too, and my meeting went late, and now I have to get dinner on the table, so if you want anything to eat, you'll help me out here." The pots crash more loudly.

"All right, all right, I'll go. Where's his practice?"

"Cherry Street Park. Today's my day to carpool, so you'll have to drop off two other boys, Hunter and Evan. You need to be there in half an hour. Thanks." Now her head's in the refrigerator.

"OK." I take the stairs two at a time, grab a quick shower and change into a pair of shorts and a MONROE HIGH SCHOOL VARSITY SOCCER T-shirt from my bedroom floor. A little wrinkled, but not smelly—passable. I'm starving, so I snag a bag of pretzels from the pantry to eat on the way, and then stop in the laundry room and shove a load of really rank soccer clothes into the washer. I'm feeling in a helpful mood. Then I start up the minivan, plug my iPhone into the console, and hit the road.

The park is on the other side of town, and I decide to drive through the center of town instead of taking the bypass. It takes a little longer, especially now during rush hour, if you can call it that, but there'll be a lot of people hanging out and I like the scenic route. Since this is a college town, the downtown has a lot of restaurants and shops and even a few art galleries, along with several bars frequented by the college students. The sidewalks are wide to accommodate pedestrians and bikes and to encourage shopping. A lot of kids from the high school hang out on the main street after school.

I'm stopped at a red light jamming out, rapping my fingers to the beat on the steering wheel, and checking out the crowd to see if I know anyone, when I see Will's dad coming out of a restaurant. I'm about to roll down my window to call out to him when I see that he's not alone. He's holding the door open for a young woman, which would be OK, except that it's not OK. Something about the way they're acting gives me a sick feeling in the pit of my stomach. My greeting dies in my throat. She's very attractive and much younger than Will's mom, and she's laughing and leaning into Will's dad in a flirty kind of way. They turn onto the sidewalk, and Will's dad puts his hand in the small of her back to guide her around a group of students. Then a car honks behind me, and I look up to see that the light's changed to green.

I drive the rest of the way to Drew's practice on autopilot. *Did I just see Will's dad with another woman?* I'm pretty freaked, since I've known Mr. Asplunth since grade school and spent countless hours at their house hanging out or sleeping over. He's almost like an uncle to me. And what do I say to Will? *Should* I say anything to Will? I didn't really see anything, anyway, right? They were out in broad daylight in the middle of town where anyone could see them. I know I'm trying to convince myself because my clenched gut is telling me it wasn't right.

Drew's team is still practicing when I pull into the gravel parking lot, so I park the car and get out to watch the eight-year-olds play. I walk to the front of the van and lean against the hood, still warm from the engine. The boys are scrimmaging; half of them have on orange pinnies over their T-shirts. At this age, they're still not doing much in the way of plays or strategies, but it's way better than the five-year-olds, who all go after the ball in a bunch like a swarm of bees.

That thought brings me back to Will's dad again. He was our coach for a couple years before we started playing travel soccer. We would've been just about Drew's age. I think about Will's mom . . . and then I don't want to think about Will's mom. *Shit.* I kick at a clod of dirt. It's so dry that it bursts into a cloud of dust.

A honking noise brings my eyes overhead. A group of Canada geese in *V* formation flies past, low over the fields and players, honking loudly. The *V* is a bit ragged; one side is shorter than the other and a few birds straggle behind. It seems too early for them to be practicing flying south, but then I'm not sure if they ever migrate at all, as there always seem to be geese on all the ponds and lakes, even in winter. I start thinking about what makes them fly together like that. I mean, some of it must be instinct, but how do they communicate with each other while they're flying about who is going to lead and which direction to fly? Is it just by sight or do they sense something more? I remember watching a show on Nova one time that showed how, when large flocks of birds fly together, you can actually see the waves of movement roll across the flock when it changes direction and that the wave moves faster than the birds could react by simply observing their neighbor and then changing course.

The show didn't really have an explanation for it, just a lot of theories, one of which was that the birds knew what to do from observing the birds farther away in the flock, but I didn't think that made sense. The wave moved so uniformly across the flock, I just felt like the birds had to be communicating another way.

The coach stops play and calls the boys over. They get drinks from their water bottles and gather their gear while he talks to them, and then they separate into groups of two and three and start walking slowly toward the parking lot and the waiting parents.

"Hey, Drew, over here!" I call out and wave. He sees me and starts running over. There's enough of an age difference between us that I have a sort of demigod status in his eyes. Even more so now that I'm on the varsity team.

"Eriiiccccc!" he calls out, slamming into me and encircling my waist with his arms. It's good to be loved.

"Hey, buddy," I say, and give him a playful wrestle. Two other boys come running over.

"Are you on the varsity soccer team at Monroe?" one of them asks.

"Yup," I answer.

"That is so cool," the other boy says.

"He's the goalkeeper," Drew says proudly, standing with his arm around me possessively.

"You guys should come to the game tomorrow night. We play Northbrook at seven o'clock." I slide the doors of the van open with the remote. "Hop in." They scramble in, chattering about going to the game. I pull out of the parking lot and hear honking coming from behind us. The geese are taking another practice run, and as they come into view and glide past, higher in the sky, I see that this time they form a perfect *V*.

6

ONE COOL THING about being on the soccer team is that we all wear our jerseys to school before home games. We don't get the same attention as the football players, but it still feels good to walk the halls and have people know that I'm on the team. The real reason for wearing our jerseys is to drum up attendance from the student body at the games. My clothing selection is pertinent today, as Cole and I are designing a survey for psych class on "What Do You Find Attractive," or, as Cole calls it, the "Hot or Not" survey. We have to put together a poster with charts and present our findings to the class.

"So, we need to come up with four or five articles of clothing or appearance for both guys and girls as our 'hot-o-meter' selection criteria," Cole says. The class has broken into teams of two, and we've pushed our desks close so we can work together.

"OK . . . like shorts and jeans and T-shirts?" I ask since that's mostly what I wear.

"No, everybody wears shorts and T-shirts. We have to come up with things that are more ambiguous, so we can get a variety of responses for our graph."

"What about lipstick, bright red lipstick? Some guys like it, but I think it's overdoing it."

"That's a good one." Cole writes it down on his list. "Uggs are definitely not hot. We should add them to the list."

"Yeah, but I don't think any guy would find them hot and we want things that are not so certain."

"You're right. Yoga pants, perhaps? They're only hot if worn by a girl with the right figure." He makes an hourglass shape in the air.

"Right. What about guys. We need more for guys." I look at him for ideas.

"How about clean cut versus hipster or jock?"

"Great!" That gives me an idea for another category. "We could do beard or clean shaven."

"Oh, I like that one. The survey results should be interesting."

We keep brainstorming and come up with a pretty good list for the survey. The fun part is the data gathering, where we get to ask all the students their opinions. At lunch we ask the guys sitting at our table the questions about girls. The responses are pretty mixed, which is what we'd hoped for, but the general consensus is that yoga pants are hot, and Uggs are not. No real surprises there.

After school, we do light warm-ups to get ready for the game. JV plays at five, and varsity has to watch their game from the stands, so now I'm suited up and sitting with the guys on the top of the bleachers, chilling out until our game. The sun is high in a perfectly blue sky and it feels awesome—not as hot as it has been. There's pretty good student attendance for JV. It's Friday night, which helps, and there's always a core group of soccer fans that comes to the games. More if it's on a Friday or Saturday, and if it's a tight game, like tonight. Of course, the parents are out in force. Some of them are pretty rabid fans. Yelling at the players and refs from the sidelines. I like it that my parents come to my games, but I want this to be for me, not them. Fortunately, they don't yell a lot. I'm trying not to think too much about whether I'm starting or not, but I'm definitely nervous. Brett is sitting with some of the Seniors at the far end of the risers looking unconcerned. Paul's right in front of me, and I have to comment on the fact that he's spiked his black hair into a mohawk.

"I didn't know you have Native American blood," I say, as I lightly touch my hand to the pointy tops of his hair.

Paul turns to look at me, his almond eyes squinting even more into the sun. "One hundred percent Asian American, man. I just thought the 'hawk looked aggressive. Psych them out, y'know?"

"You definitely look scary," I say, deadpan.

"Yeah, well imagine how scary you're gonna look when we make regionals and we shave your head."

"Sorry, no can do. I'm like Samson with my strength in my hair." I laugh. I turn my attention to the game. "If their varsity plays as good as their JV is playing, it looks like Coach is right about Northbrook being tough this year." Our team is holding their own, but its zero–zero at halftime.

"They're always tough. It's their All-State striker we're gonna have to mark. You'll need to be on your best game." He says it matter of factly and looks away. I wonder what he knows, but I don't say anything more.

About halfway through the second half, Coach Vince calls us down from the stands, and we file down the aisles, our cleats ringing loudly on the metal risers. "Go Monroe!" call out some of the spectators when we pass by. As we're walking around the field, I see my parents, Drew and his two friends from soccer, and Marcie and her friend Sara, arriving. It's like the whole entourage. No pressure here or anything, but I'm glad they came. They're here early to watch the warm-ups.

"Hey," I say casually and stop to see them.

"Hey, bud," my dad says. "Just do your best and have fun tonight." He cuffs me lightly on the shoulder.

"Have a good game, honey," says my mom.

"Are you starting tonight?" Drew just comes right out with it.

"We'll see. Let's hope so."

"I know you're starting. You're the best." It's good to be loved.

"Thanks, buddy. Cheer us on, OK? I gotta go."

I'm by myself as I walk the rest of the way toward the bench. Even though I'm trying not to think about it, I want to start so badly. I feel like my whole soccer career has been leading up to this. When I reach the bench, Coach Swenson calls me over to where he's standing with Brett. *This is it.*

"OK, guys. Eric is starting in goal tonight, but I want you to understand that the position is still wide open. It's either of yours to win. Got it?" He looks first at me and then at Brett. We nod. "Brett, you warm him up." He tosses Brett a ball, turns, and walks away.

Whoa—I'm starting. Suddenly, I have a big knot in my gut. I mean, I'm totally psyched that I'm starting and I feel like the top of my head is going to pop off from excitement, but I'm also kind of freaked out. The way Coach Swenson just sprang it on me that I'm starting right before the game and that I still have to fight for the spot doesn't give me much time to get my head around it. I'm also not really sure what to say to Brett. He can't be feeling too hot right now, so I can't really celebrate and I can't say I'm sorry, since I'm not sorry, and that would sound stupid anyway, so I don't say anything. And it's clear that my starting isn't set in stone. I have to prove myself in the game, so I know Brett will be breathing down my back. We put on our gloves and walk together over to the goal in silence. I get positioned in the goal, and Brett starts lobbing some easy shots my way. One of the ball boys collects the balls and sends them back to Brett. After a few minutes, he smiles and says, "Are you feeling warmed up now Horton? 'Cause you better be set for what comes next. We want you to be ready for Northbrook," and then he sends a screamer right at my head. I manage to block the shot, but it's too fast to catch, so the ball drops to the ground at my feet. I pick it up and punt it back to him.

"Hell yeah!" I say, as he sends one into the lower left corner and I dive for it.

THE STANDS HAVE filled up while we were warming up, and the crowd is jamming to the music blasting out of the loudspeakers. It's almost game time. I line up with the other starters, and we jog across the center of the field toward the stands. I keep my expression serious, which isn't too hard, since I'm trying to focus, but I have to admit that it feels amazing to be starting. The crowd cheers for us, and I scan their faces for someone I know. I see Cole sitting near Will's girlfriend Bonnie and her group of friends and then I look again and see that he's sitting next to Renee. *Why am I not surprised?*

My family is sitting at the top of the bleachers, and my dad is standing up and shaking hands with Will's dad. I don't see Will's mom, which is weird since she comes to all his games, but I tell myself that it doesn't mean anything.

The music stops and the announcer calls out the names and positions of the starters. When he calls out, "Number one, Eric Horton, goalkeeper," I step forward and wave. Drew and his friends are yelling and jumping around. I sneak a look at Renee. She's clapping, and, next to her, Cole is whooping and pumping his fist in the air. Then we turn and jog back. Now comes the real stuff. Game time.

Monroe wins the toss, so we have the kickoff. I orient myself in the goal, hoping my routine will help settle my pre-game nerves. Will's also starting. He's in position at center back, so it's our defensive unit, just like we wanted. The ref blows his whistle, and the game begins. Our forwards take the ball downfield, making quick, short passes, maneuvering toward Northbrook's goal. The action stays at the other end of the field for a while and then Paul takes a shot . . . but it's wide left of the goal.

The Northbrook keeper retrieves the ball and takes the goal kick, sending it across the center line into my side of the field. I keep my eyes on the play, ready to move, but Will is right there and passes it to one of our midfielders, who takes it down to the other end again. Then, one of the Northbrook players intercepts a pass, gets possession, and starts running toward me with the ball. It's their star striker and he's fast. Really fast. He beats our defenders. Will is running with him, trying to force him wide, to cut the angle, but he's losing ground. It's all on me. *Quick! Think! Come out or hold the line?* I start to come out and then question myself and stop. Hesitate. Now I'm in no-man's land. *Shit!* He's too far away for me to dive at his feet, and I'm too far out of the goal to block a shot. He chips the ball over my head. I turn and see it bounce into the goal. *Damn!*

I can't believe it. That was mine to save and I totally blew it. The worst thing about being a keeper is that one mistake can mean a goal. You have to act on instinct, without hesitation. The field players make mistakes all the time, but they don't always lead to a goal.

Will is walking toward me. I don't even want to talk to him, I'm so mad. Getting scored on this early in the game is really bad. It sucks the energy from the team. Now we're down one. We have to score twice to win.

"Hey, man, shake it off." Will catches up to me as I walk back to the goal. "We can do this. You just need to get your head in the game."

"Yeah. I totally overthought that one. What a shitty goal." Even though I did it in practice, I don't like to act mad or upset on the field, because it makes me look weak, so I try to look confident and walk tall back into position.

I get back in the goal and go through my routine. Then I close my eyes for a minute, relax my shoulders, let out my breath and try to empty my head. I visualize making saves like the sports psychology stuff I've been reading. The whistle blows. I'm ready.

Northbrook takes the ball, and, high on adrenaline from scoring, they come out charging. Our defenders fight them off, but the ball stays on our side of the field. Now the play is moving closer . . . a shot is coming, *I know it*. I see the ball zooming toward me, over my head. I jump and reach and just tip the ball up, but instead of going up and over the top of the net, it hits the crossbar and bounces out in front of the goal. *Another shot!* I dive right and block the second shot with my body. It ricochets off me right at the feet of the Northbrook striker. He settles it and shoots . . . but I'm up on my knees and I lunge left and grab the ball, pulling it in close. My heart is hammering in my chest. My teammates are yelling. The crowd is screaming. *Three saves!*

"Way to go, big guy!" Will yells.

"Awesome save, Eric!" someone else calls out.

I walk slowly to the edge of the penalty box, savoring the moment. I bounce the ball three times and punt it so it arcs high in the sky across the center line to the other end of the field. We end up winning two to one. Making those three saves in a row really helped pump up our team and deflate Northbrook. I didn't let them score on me again.

Coach Swenson talks to us for a few minutes after the game, and then we grab our gear and walk toward the locker room entrance, where the fans are waiting to congratulate us. I texted Renee that I would meet her here after the game and then we would figure out what we wanted to do, so I'm scoping out the crowd looking for her. She's standing over to one side with Cole and Bonnie. As I walk over to them, some of the fans congratulate me on my saves, and I stop and say goodbye to my family. Will has gone over to talk to his dad, and I can see that they're arguing.

"Hey," I say to Renee when I reach them. "Do you mind waiting here a few minutes while I take a quick shower? I thought we could get something to eat in town."

"Sure," she says, smiling. My heart does a flip.

"We'll wait here with her," Cole volunteers. "Then we can all go together."

"OK. Maybe." I really want to be alone with Renee for our first "date." "What's up with Will and his dad?" I nod in their direction. I have a bad feeling about it.

"There's something going on with them, but I don't know what," Bonnie says, frowning and shaking her head, which makes her blond curls jump. "Will's really pissed at him."

Maybe I know. "I'll be right back." The locker room isn't my first choice for personal hygiene since it's pretty gross, but it's all there is, so I shower and change and am back out again within ten minutes. The crowd has thinned out by now and it's getting dark. Renee, Cole, and Bonnie are sitting in the grass.

"We were thinking we'd all go to Bub's Burgers," Cole says.

"OK, but maybe Renee and I could meet you there." I look at Renee. "Do you want to walk over? It's not too far."

"Yes, I'd love to," she says, getting up and brushing the grass off her shorts.

It's not totally dark yet, more like dusk, but all the street lights are already on in the parking lot. There's an older residential neighborhood between the high school and downtown, and I steer us in that direction instead of the taking the main drag so we can walk through the quieter streets. The buzzing of cicadas rises and falls in a wave of sound all around us, and the smell of freshly mown grass scents the warm night air. We pass a group of kids playing kick the can in the dark. I'm very conscious of Renee beside me. Even though we don't know each other very well, I feel a connection to her.

"So, how do you like living in the States?" I ask.

"I've visited before, but living here is different. Everything is so big! The houses and cars are bigger, the streets are wider, and the supermarket is enormous. Even the people are bigger—I mean, taller," she adds quickly.

"Just admit it, you mean fatter," I laugh.

"No, really, I didn't!" She stops and puts a hand on my arm. I think she's afraid she's offended me.

"It's OK," I say. "We're pretty well aware of it."

"Well, some people are fatter, but Americans really are taller. Like you," she says softly. She's looking up at me. The top of her head barely comes up to my chin. We're almost facing each other, stopped on the sidewalk. I look down at her and her eyes meet mine. We stand there for a moment and I get that feeling of *knowing*, like I know her more than I possibly could already, and then my eyes travel down her face to her slightly parted lips. I can't help wondering what it would be like to kiss her. I take a breath and quickly turn away. It's too soon for that. I start walking again and she falls in place beside me.

"It helps to be tall in the goal," I say to break the spell.

"You were great tonight. Those saves you made in the first half changed the game in our favor."

"Thanks. You seem to know about soccer."

"It's extremely popular in Europe, more like a religion. Everyone watches it."

"Was it hard for you to leave your friends behind to come here?"

"Yes and no. I could have stayed in France and lived with my grandparents, but it's exciting to come here. An adventure. I also wanted to be with my family."

"Do you have brothers and sisters?"

"A younger sister. What about you?"

"A younger brother and a younger sister." Even going at a slow pace, we've reached the end of the neighborhood. If we cross the street and continue we'll almost be at the restaurant. I'm not ready to join the others yet, so I ask, "Are you hungry or do you want to keep walking?"

"I ate something earlier, so I'm fine. Let's keep walking."

"Good." I smile at her and turn right at the corner down another residential street.

"So, where was I in my questioning? I know—what is your favorite thing to do?"

"Am I being interrogated?"

"Yes. Do you mind?"

"No, as long as I get equal time. I would say my favorite thing to do right now is painting and drawing. Last year it was sculpting."

"So you're an artist. Is that what you'd like to do when you grow up?" I make quotation marks in the air.

"I think so. I'm just not sure what type of art." We pass under a street lamp and it abruptly goes out.

I surprise myself by saying, "That happens to me a lot."

"What happens?" she asks.

"You'll probably think this is weird, but street lights and lights in parking garages often go on or off when I go under them."

"Really?" She looks at me quizzically.

"I've never really told anyone about it because it's hard to explain. I mean, a light going on or off isn't really a big deal, but it happens to me so much that I started noticing it. Kind of strange." I laugh self-consciously.

"It actually reminds me of a scientist my father knows, although for him it's much worse. My dad says that every time this guy comes into the lab, the instruments start to go haywire and their experiments get messed up."

"No kidding? That makes what happens to me seem less bizarre. It must make it hard for that guy to do his job."

"You would think so. My dad says it may have something to do with his energy field. Maybe you have a strong energy field, too."

"I've wondered if it might be something like that because of the electricity. So, do you know anything about the remote viewing studies your dad is doing? Will and I are thinking about signing up."

"I've done some of them myself, but not the paired studies. They're pretty interesting. He's found that bonded pairs do better at intuiting what the other partner is thinking or doing than randomly paired subjects, which makes sense. You should come tomorrow. One of his graduate assistants can't be there, so I'm helping my dad."

"OK, I'll talk to Will. That would be great."

We turn a corner and are right down the street from Bub's.

"Do you mind if we join the others at Bub's now? This American boy is starving and I could use a burger!" I pat my hand on my stomach, which, thankfully, is flat.

"Of course. Didn't you say something about ice cream?"

"They've got the best in town."

The restaurant is crowded with families and teens out on the town. I see Will, Bonnie, and Cole sitting in a booth at the back of the restaurant. Will and Bonnie are on one side, and Will has his arm draped across the back of the booth behind her. Renee slides into the seat next to Cole on the other side of the booth, and I sit next to her so she's sandwiched between us.

"It's about time you guys got here," Will says. "We're already done."

"I can see that." Their plates, with the remains of their burgers, fries, and milkshakes, cover the table. "We took the long way. We're going to order something now if you want to hang out a while longer."

"No problem," Cole says. He's leaning on his elbow looking at Renee. "So, Renee, did Eric tell you about the survey we're doing for psych class?" The waitress comes and we order our food.

"No, he didn't mention it."

"It's called 'Hot or Not.'"

"Hmm. Interesting." She's smiling warily at him, not sure where this is going.

"We're asking students whether they think different articles of clothing or characteristics are 'hot or not' and then graphing the results. It's very scientific."

Bonnie snorts and laughs, making her blond curls bounce. "Ha! They're really just using it to find out what girls think is hot."

"Well, of course. We also want to communicate what guys think is not hot."

"Like what?" asks Renee.

"The survey results show that the number one in the Not Hot category for us are Ugg boots." Cole says.

"Also, too much make-up. That is definitely not hot," says Will.

"What about what girls think is not hot?" says Bonnie. She's leaning forward. "How about BO and ratty clothes? Not attractive."

"We can add those to the list," Cole says. "All right, let's switch gears to what is hot. Renee, what about you? Anything that you find particularly attractive?" he asks with a deceptively nonchalant air. I was waiting for this. I figured he'd been leading up to something like this all along.

"Well, I think someone who has good manners and is confident is attractive," she says, skirting the question.

"Ah, those are good traits, and I believe that your date, Mr. Horton here, possesses them, but what about appearance? Hair, for instance. What do you think of Eric's long soccer hair?" He reaches behind her to ruffle my hair, and I bat his hand away.

I feel like I should step in to deflect Cole's question, but I also want to know what she thinks, so I don't say anything right away. Renee turns to look directly at me, smiles and says, "Hot. Definitely hot." Without missing a beat. I smile back and think,

Ha! She's not shy. Will lets out a low whistle. Then I feel the heat start to rise in my face and I'm afraid I'm going to blush, so I say, "OK, let's move off of that topic."

Fortunately, the waitress brings my burger and fries and Renee's milkshake right then. Will says, "I heard there's a party tonight at Todd Sloan's. Do you guys want to go?"

"That's kind of a party crowd, isn't it?" says Bonnie, a crease forming between her blue eyes.

"Maybe," says Will, stealing a fry off my plate, "but come on, it'll be fun and we don't have to partake. Anyway, one beer never hurt anyone. Hey, we *won* tonight! I want to enjoy the moment."

I turn to Renee. "Do you want to go? It'll be crowded and noisy."

"I don't mind either way, really."

"Well, if you don't mind, I'd rather skip it. I'm beat and it'll just be a bunch of people standing around drinking." To Will, I say, "Renee says that Dr. Auberge is doing the remote viewing study tomorrow and we can go. We have to be there by nine."

"That's cool. Don't worry, I'll be by to pick you up at 8:30."

After we finish our food, Will, Cole, and Bonnie leave to go to the party, and Renee and I walk back through the neighborhood to the high school and my car. It's nice just to be with her and talk. I feel really comfortable around her. A party isn't a good place to get to know someone, and I really am tired. When I pull up to her driveway to drop her off, I'm trying to decide if I should kiss her goodnight, and what kind of a kiss it should be. As I put the car in park and turn toward her, she lays her hand on my chest and leans into me. She stops with her lips just inches from mine. She can probably feel my heart pounding in my chest. I look into her eyes a moment, then reach my hand to the side of her head and close the distance between our lips. It's a soft kiss, just a momentary touching of our lips, but it's unreal. I don't want to rush things, so I lift my head and then lean my forehead against hers and whisper, "Goodnight, Renee. I'll see you tomorrow."

"Good night," she says. "I had a great time."

7

THE FEAR IS strong, but the sense of urgency and foreboding is stronger. I have to act quickly or something terrible will happen. But what? What do I need to do? It's all confusion. Then comes the explosion. And heat. Intense, searing heat. Someone is screaming. It's too late! Oh God!

I wake up in my bed gripped with fear and drenched in sweat, the sheets wrapped around my legs. I lie there shaking and breathing hard while the realization sinks in that it was another nightmare. Not real. *Holy shit.* I roll onto my side and curl into a ball. *Breathe. In and out. Calm down.* I get up and walk shakily down the dark hallway to the bathroom, get a drink, splash water on my face, and lean against the sink, feeling the cool, hard counter beneath my hands. The details of the dream aren't clear; just the fear and the urgency and the tearing, ripping explosion. Even that is starting to fade at the edges and slip away, thankfully. When I get back in bed, I concentrate on thinking about Renee and our kiss to chase away any remnants of the nightmare. This time, my dreams are peaceful.

DREW IS ALREADY downstairs watching cartoons when I come down for breakfast. I took a quick shower this morning, basically to make sure my hair isn't sticking out all over the place, and I want to have a bowl of cereal or something before Will picks me up.

"Hey, buddy, what's up?" I ask as I sit down on the couch next to Drew and put my bowl and the gallon of milk on the coffee table.

"Eric!" He pummels me with his fists and I retaliate by grabbing his wrists and pinning him to the cushions.

"You're doomed." I transfer his wrists to one hand and tickle him mercilessly with the other. Just a little brotherly love.

"OK, OK, stop!" Drew says between gasps of laughter.

"All right, truce. I need to scarf down this cereal. What're you doing today?" I pour cereal into the bowl and fill it up with milk.

"I've got a soccer game at 9:30. Can you come watch me?"

"Sorry little dude, I have to be somewhere, but maybe I can go to the next one."

Mom comes into the kitchen and starts the coffee maker. "Good morning, guys." She comes over to stand by the couch. "Eric, I would really rather you didn't eat in the family room, and please put the milk away next time." She picks up the jug. "How about cereal with strawberries for you, Drew?"

"Sorry," I say. "I'm going with Will to be part of a study with the physics professor I told you about."

"That's fine. We've got Drew's game this morning and your dad already took Marcie to school to catch the bus for her cross-country meet. We won't be back till this afternoon."

My cell buzzes in my pocket. I pull it out and see a text from Will: IN THE DRIVEWAY. RIGHT ON TIME.

"I gotta go. Will's here." I get up and give Drew one last tickle.

"Bring your bowl and the cereal box into the kitchen please!" she calls out.

"Right. Will do." I grab the empty bowl and box and leave them on the counter. Not exactly put away, but in the right vicinity. "See you later."

"You missed a wicked party last night!" Will says as I climb into the Taurus. "A lot of guys from the team were there and everyone was dancing. It was crazy."

"Late night?" I notice he's drinking a highly caffeinated energy drink.

"What are you, my mom now?" he replies with an edge to his voice, which surprises me because usually Will's so easy going. "I was home by one. I'll take a nap this afternoon, if it'll make you happy." I'm a little ticked at this, so I say, "I don't care what you do. I just wondered if you were up late. Don't get shitty with me."

"I just don't need you checking up on me, OK." He takes a swig of the energy drink. "So, do you know where we're going?"

"Yeah, it's in a lab at the physics department at the university." I'm still pissed about Will's remark. We talk about last night's game the rest of the way to the university—an easy subject.

When we get there, Renee is checking people in at a table in front of the lab. Her hair is pulled back into a ponytail, and she's wearing a lab coat, which gives her a sexy librarian look. She's talking to a man and a woman who I guess are married or boyfriend and girlfriend. When she's done, she turns to us.

"Hi, I'm glad you came." I love that she really looks happy to see us *(me?)*.

"Hey. You look very official."

"Why, thank you." She pulls the lapels of the coat together and makes a serious face. "It helps people to know I'm part of the staff."

"How does this work, and what will we actually be doing?" Will asks.

"It's a remote viewing study with bonded pairs, as opposed to random pairs. You'll be in separate rooms, and one of you will be viewing images on a computer screen. The other one will try to identify what he is seeing on the screen. We're looking at both the ability of the viewer to send or communicate the image and the ability of the receiver to identify it." She hands us each some papers. "You need to fill out these questionnaires before you start, and you'll each be paid twenty dollars for the half hour session."

"Are you measuring psychic ability, or mind reading, or what exactly?" asks Will, a bit skeptically.

Renee either doesn't notice his tone or chooses to ignore it. "You could call it that. My father is studying the degree to which people are able to tap into the consciousness of others and how the relationship between people affects our ability to communicate in that way." She points to a table and chairs further down the hallway. "You can complete the questionnaires over there." She turns to the people who arrived behind us.

We sit down at the table, and Will says in a low voice, "Seems like a weird thing for a physicist to be studying, don't you think?" I kind of agree, but I just shrug.

The questionnaire starts out with basic stuff like name, age, address, and my relationship to my bonded pair—*not so good at the moment, I think*—and then asks a lot of questions about experiences and how frequently they happen. 'Do you experience coincidences? Seldom, Sometimes, Often.' *Seldom.* 'Do you ever get a feeling of déjà-vu? Seldom, Sometimes, Often.' *Hmmm, seldom.* 'Do you ever know that something is going to happen before it does? Seldom, Sometimes, Often.' *Do I? Yeah, when I'm in the goal and I feel like I know where the shot is going to go.* I answer 'sometimes' because it doesn't always happen, and I'm not sure if it isn't just athletic instinct or something like that. The next question really throws me, though. 'Do you ever dream about something that later comes true?' *No!*—the word immediately and strongly fills my head.

I've had the explosion dream twice, but so what? It doesn't mean it's coming true. I'm just not going there. I mark 'Seldom' and move on to the next question.

We give the completed questionnaires to Renee, and she has us wait at the table for one of the graduate assistants to come get us for our session. After about fifteen minutes, Dr. Auberge himself comes out of the door to the lab. He talks to Renee for a minute and then comes over to Will and me.

He's dressed in slacks and a polo shirt. I guess he doesn't need the lab coat to look like a scientist. He extends his hand for each of us to shake, and we both automatically stand up.

Will shakes his hand and says, "Hi, I'm Will Asplunth."

"I'm Eric Horton," I say, as we shake hands. "You were a guest lecturer in our AP Enviro science class."

"Yes, Renee told me you were coming today. And you are also teammates on the varsity soccer team?"

"Eric's the goalkeeper and I'm the center back. We've played together for years."

"Ah, the defensive team. Well, I'm pleased that you've decided to participate in the study. I wanted to get some younger subjects, and your bonded pair relationship is unique. Not the usual romantic or family relationship. If you come with me, I'll bring you back to the study rooms, and my graduate assistant will get you set up."

We follow him to the door and pass Renee on our way. "I guess it's our turn," I say to her.

"OK. I'll probably be gone when you're finished, so I'll see you later." She gives a little wave goodbye. *Damn.* There goes my chance to casually ask her what she's doing the rest of the weekend. Now I'll have to text her. The whole guy making the first move thing really sucks. Although, I guess it would suck if you were a girl and you thought you had to wait for a guy to ask you out. Not that girls don't do a lot of asking out, they do, and frankly I like being asked out by a girl. It's just that most of the time, guys are expected to do it.

Dr. Auberge takes us to a small office where a really tall, lanky guy in a lab coat is sitting at a desk in front of a computer. His arms are so long that a good three inches of his wrists stick out from the sleeves of his coat.

"This is Stephen. He'll be helping you from here," says Dr. Auberge.

"You guys can have a seat." Stephen gestures to the two wooden chairs in front of the desk. He finishes typing something into the computer. "All right, so here's how this works. Each of you will be in separate, soundproof rooms with computers that are not linked to each other in any way. One of you will be the 'sender,' who will be viewing images on the computer screen. A new image will appear every two minutes. The sender is basically supposed to look at the image and think about it and try in a very relaxed way to communicate the image to the other person, who is the 'receiver.' The receiver will have one minute to get impressions of what he might be receiving and one minute to register what the impressions are on a brief questionnaire on the computer. The session lasts thirty minutes, so there will be fifteen images in total. Don't work too hard at it, but try to stay focused. Any questions?" We look at each other and shake our heads.

"Nope, I think we've got it," says Will.

"Right. Who wants to be the sender?" Stephen looks back and forth between us.

"I'll do that," Will says. "It sounds like the easier job."

"Slacker," I say.

"Then you come with me first and I'll get you set up," Stephen tells Will. To me he says, "I'll be back for you in a minute." He practically leaps out of his chair and walks with a jerky, loping gait, gesturing for Will to follow.

When he comes back for me, he takes me to a small, cubbyhole room with a desk and a laptop computer.

"Your programs run separately, but we've got them both set up to run without your intervention. You just need to be in a receptive mode for one minute and then answer the questions when they come on the screen about your impressions. The screen will switch automatically. All set?"

"I think so."

"Great. See you in half an hour."

It's really quiet in the room. I can actually hear my breathing. I just sit there, chilling for a few minutes, thinking that this is a pretty easy way to make twenty bucks. Then the computer screen lights up with the words PROGRAM BEGINNING IN 10 SECONDS, and it counts down from ten to zero. When it begins, the screen is blank. This must be the first image I'm supposed to receive, so I try not to think of anything in particular and just look at the screen and try to visualize . . . something. The screen is blank, but I'm getting impressions of an X or a cross and maybe palm trees? Something tropical? I'm not really sure. After what seems like less than a minute, the questionnaire appears on the screen. I answer questions about whether the image I got was: straight or wavy; round, square, triangular or rectangular; in water or land; woods or prairie; and so on. Then I have to write a ten word description. Just as I finish, the screen goes blank and I guess I'm on to the next one. The time goes by pretty fast and before I realize I've done fifteen images, the last questionnaire disappears and the screen says SESSION COMPLETED. I stand up and stretch. I didn't really see any actual images during the session, but I did feel like I was getting something—general impressions that could have just been my own imagination, too. I have no idea if I really got anything or not. Stephen opens the door a minute later.

"You're all done," he says. Will's behind him.

"How'd we do?"

"You're the last two, so if you want to come back to the office with me and wait a minute, I'll pull up your results." I look at Will, who says, "Sure, I can wait, but if you don't get an A don't be upset. You're such an overachiever. "

"Somebody has to be," I shoot back.

We go back to the first room where we met Stephen and sit across the desk from him as he works on the computer.

"Well," he leans back in his chair. "Pretty strong results for your first time. You had a 33 percent accuracy rate. Most random pairs score 16 percent or less the first time, and bonded pairs usually don't do better than 25 percent without any training. We'll definitely want you to come back and do some more studies. Probably some individual sessions, too."

"Awesome. So does that mean that we have some sort of psychic ability?" Will says seriously, but he kicks my foot where Stephen can't see him. To me, 33 percent accuracy doesn't seem like all that big a deal, but Stephen seems to think it is. I did feel like I was getting something back in the dark room with the computer, but I don't know exactly what it was. Really, 33 percent of fifteen is only five correct. That doesn't seem like much.

"It definitely shows that you were able to communicate the images between each other. Everyone has that ability, but some people more than others. We think of it as 'enhanced consciousness.' It's a skill you can develop, too. Can you come back to the lab this week after school for more sessions?"

"We've got soccer practice every day after school; what about in the evening?" I'm not sure how I feel about having 'enhanced consciousness.' Maybe it helps to explain my soccer perceptions, but so what? What does it even mean?

"We have sessions on Thursday nights, so plan on coming at 7:00 p.m. for two hours this time. I've got you scheduled."

"Sounds good." Our chairs scrape the floor as we get up to leave. When the door to the lab closes behind us, Will says, "That wasn't what I expected at all. What does 'enhanced consciousness' have to do with alternative energy sources or the Zero Point Energy Field? Dr. Auberge is really out there with this stuff."

"Yeah, I guess. Maybe because he's on a research sabbatical he's able to investigate things that are less mainstream—more experimental or cutting edge."

"More like the lunatic fringe, but it's an easy way to make twenty bucks for a half hour's work." I don't say anything. I know I can't really talk to Will about the sports visualization stuff or the feelings I get sometimes when I'm in the goal, because he doesn't take it seriously. But what if it's a skill or ability that I can improve or develop like Stephen said? Am I already using it and I didn't even realize it? I leave the lab not feeling sure about whether I want to find out or not.

8

"It's Spicy Chicken Tuesday!" Paul says as he puts his tray down on the table and pulls out a chair next to Cole. "I love Spicy Chicken."

"I have to agree that in its first appearance on the menu, Spicy Chicken is fairly edible," says Cole.

"What do you mean, 'its first appearance?'" asks Paul.

"Dude, don't you know about the Spicy Chicken Cycle?" I ask.

"No. I'm not sure I want to know, either."

"Haven't you ever noticed that a day or two after they serve the Spicy Chicken sandwich, Oriental Spicy Chicken is on the menu, which, by the way, is still fairly tasty and in the realm of digestible, and then after that we get Spicy Chicken Balls, which I would caution you to avoid at all costs," Cole tells him.

"Hey, man, you're right! But I don't really care as long as it tastes good," Paul says, and then takes a bite of his sandwich. "Mmmm."

"You are a human garbage disposal, Paul," says Will. He's mixing up his special concoction of hot sauce and ranch dressing that he puts on practically everything he eats. "There's also a

Chuck Wagon Meat cycle that starts out as a hamburger, is served up next as Salisbury steak with gravy, and finishes the cycle as Chuck Wagon Stew. Want some of my special sauce?" he says to no one in particular and pushes a paper plate smeared with bright orange sauce into the center of the table. "It makes everything taste better."

"I'm good," I say. I try not to think too much about what's in the food they serve in the cafeteria. "So, will we get to see your dad at the coal gasification plant on tomorrow's field trip?" I ask without thinking. I regret it almost immediately when I see the laughter leave Will's face and his expression close down.

"I wouldn't know. I haven't talked to him," he replies tersely. It's clear he doesn't want to talk about it, so nobody says anything else. I'm surprised Will hasn't said anything to me about what's going on with his dad, because, obviously, there is something going on.

AFTER DINNER, I drive over to Renee's house. We're having a "homework date," and although I would've preferred to meet at a more neutral location, like the library—read, *without parents*—she invited me over to her house, so here I am. I park on the street and walk across the lawn to the front door. Her family is living in one of the houses near campus that the university keeps for visiting professors. It's in the older part of town, not far from where I live, where every house is a different style. Not like the cookie-cutter housing developments. Renee's house is a Tudor-style bungalow with timbered walls and white-washed stucco. I hesitate a minute on the front stoop, basically so I can muster my courage . . . then I take a deep breath and ring the bell. Of course, Dr. Auberge answers the door.

"Ah, hello. It's Eric, correct?" he says. "You must be here to see Renee."

"Yes, sir. We're doing homework together."

"Well, come in then." He holds open the door for me. "Renee!" he calls up the stairs. "You have a visitor!"

"OK, I need to clean up my paint and brushes. I'll be down in a minute," she replies from somewhere on the second floor.

"Come back to the kitchen. No telling how long a minute could be." *Great. One-on-one time with dad.* You'd think that I'd jump at the chance to get in good with him because of the internship, but I'm pretty sure that dating his daughter isn't one of the selection criteria. Might even count against me. "Would you like something to drink? Water, soda?" asks Dr. Auberge.

"No, thanks, I'm good." I find a spot to stand by the kitchen table and try not to look too uncomfortable.

"Please, sit down." He gestures to the table and pulls out a chair for himself. I sit on the edge of the chair nearest me, nervous because I'm wondering if I'm going to get the "potential boyfriend" grilling. I want to be ready to jump up and leave as soon as Renee comes down, but he says, "Stephen told me about your results on the remote viewing study. Impressive for your first session without any training. Also, the fact that you and your friend are not a couple. One or both of you has a very well developed enhanced consciousness."

Here's the enhanced consciousness again. "Uh, what do you mean?" I stutter out. Not the direction I expected the conversation to go.

"Well, usually for subjects who have a high score initially, we find that it's not the first time they've experienced enhanced consciousness. It might be that they have premonitions or maybe coincidences occur frequently for them. Or it could be more like feelings of déjà-vu or dreams or that they are more perceptive of the feelings of people around them. Most likely other things, too, that they aren't even fully aware of." I just stare at him for a minute. I think my mouth might even be hanging open.

"Is that true for you?" He looks at me inquiringly. It's as if he knows something about me that I didn't even fully recognize myself. I'm a little apprehensive, but also curious.

Cautiously I say, "Yeah, I guess I've had some of those things happen, but I've never thought much about it." I try to shrug it off.

"What sort of things do you experience?" He's leaning back in his chair, apparently having a casual conversation, but the way he's focused on me makes me think that he's intently listening. I figure I might as well tell him about the soccer stuff.

"Sometimes when I'm in the goal, it's almost like a thought pops into my head, and I suddenly know where the shot will be going or which way I should dive. I've always thought it was athletic instinct or something like that. I've tried out some sports psychology stuff about visualizing the outcome you want, so I figured maybe it had something to do with that."

"It could be instinctive athleticism or that you are subconsciously reading the behavior of the other players, or," he pauses for emphasis, "you could be tapping into the Collective Consciousness."

"What's that?" I feel like *The Twilight Zone*'s theme song should be playing in the background.

"It's called many things: the Akashic Record, the Universal Field of Consciousness, and by some, God. Many Eastern religions believe that we are all connected to each other and to what you could call God or higher consciousness by our thoughts and that thoughts have power, or even energy. Science is just now recognizing the power of thought. As you said, visualization is used frequently in sports, but there is much more to it than that." I'm thinking that I am in store for a really out-there conversation with Dr. Auberge, but I'm saved when Renee comes into the kitchen and puts her hand lightly on my shoulder. I didn't hear her come in so it startles me a little. The conversation with Dr. Auberge was getting pretty intense. At some deep level it resonates with me, but at the same time, thinking that there's a Universal Field of Consciousness seems straight out of a science fiction movie. It's hard to believe it could actually be real.

"I hope you're not overwhelming Eric with your theories, Papa. I don't want to scare him off," she says with a nervous laugh. "Anyway, we need to get started on something a little more practical—US History. I'm way behind the other students and I need help!"

"Not to worry, Renee, I barely touched the surface." Dr. Auberge places his palms on his thighs and stands up. "I enjoyed talking with you, Eric." He smiles and extends his hand for me to shake. "I'll see you in the lab again, I hope, and we can talk more then."

"Uh, yeah." I shake his hand and then grab my backpack and quickly follow Renee into the dining room. I can't say that I'm not intrigued by what he was saying, but thoughts having power? What the hell?

We sit down at the table and Renee says, "So are you totally 'freaked-out,' as you Americans say, now that you've had a chat with my papa about thoughts being things?" She's smiling and acting lighthearted, but there's a tenseness in the set of her shoulders, and her smile seems uncertain.

I don't want her to think that I'm not open to new ideas, but I also want to be authentic with her that this is a bit weird for me, so I say, "It is a little out there, but it's not the first time I've heard about something like it. I've read some sports psychology, and my mom's an archaeologist and anthropologist. She's told us about how some of the aboriginal people she studies seem to have a sort of group consciousness and can even predict future events. I just never thought about it in terms of something that relates to me personally. What do you mean exactly that 'thoughts are things,' and what is the Akashic Record?"

She sighs. "I didn't really want to get into this right away, but here goes. Just remember that *you* asked *me*. Thoughts are things means that our thoughts are energy; both creative energy and electrical energy. So when someone says that thoughts have power, they mean that your thoughts have the power to turn what you are thinking into reality, and also that thoughts literally have power in that they are a source of energy that can be measured."

"But everyone knows that thoughts can turn into something real. First you have an idea, then you act on the idea and then it's real." I know this isn't what she really means, but I just can't help playing devil's advocate.

"That's true, but the theory is that if a person is able to harness their thoughts and access the Collective Consciousness to focus on a goal or objective, then the step where action is required is skipped. The thought itself is what makes it happen."

"As in 'mind over matter?'"

"Pretty much, yes."

"I guess I already know that on some level, because of what happens sometimes to me in the goal and what I've read about studies done with athletes. So much of sports is mental. There was one study where they used three groups of athletes training for the same event." I drum my fingers on the table, trying to recall the article. "Two of the groups used visualization and one just trained. The groups that visualized winning *both* performed better than the one that only trained—even the group that only visualized and didn't train at all. They concluded that visualizing success was as important as training, if not more so. Still, the Collective Consciousness? What is that?"

I'm sitting with my backpack unopened on the floor, but Renee has her US History book out and a spiral notebook open on the table in front of her. I get the impression that she would rather move on to studying. "If you don't want to talk about it, that's OK," I say, and start unzipping my backpack.

"It's not so much that I don't want to talk about it, but I don't want to put you off. Not everyone is comfortable with these ideas." Her green eyes gaze at me questioningly. She's basically asking if I think she and her dad are nuts or something, so I reach for her hand resting on the table.

"Whenever something seems too different or too wild to believe, I think about when my dad takes us out to the country with his telescope. Once you get away from the city lights you can see an amazing number of stars, even with your naked eye."

I turn her hand over and lightly trace a line on her palm, starting at her wrist and ending between her thumb and index finger. "It makes me realize that the universe is unbelievably huge and filled with things we can't even begin to know or understand."

She smiles and gives my hand a little squeeze. It travels through my fingers, up my arm, and lodges in my chest, making me catch my breath. I'd say almost anything for that feeling.

"OK," she says softly, and her face relaxes. "The Collective Consciousness is all of the thought energy from everything in the universe, like an underlying current of energy connecting everything together, and the Akashic record is like a vast library of all the thoughts and information that ever existed or ever will exist." She stops and looks at me for my reaction. I look down at her hand, still clasped in both of my mine. Her nails are perfect ovals, and the skin covering the tiny bones and muscle and sinew that make up her hand is smooth and unblemished. I am reminded of how amazing even the things we take for granted really are. The human hand is at once beautiful and miraculous. It's miraculous that we even exist at all, really. That the world exists. How different is it to consider that there could be truth to what she's saying?

Thoughts are things. Currents of thought energy. A library of thoughts.

We're both quiet for a moment as I process what she's said, and then a thought occurs to me. "So does this have anything to do with the Universal Energy Field?"

"Yes," she says, "they're related, maybe the same, but I don't think I could explain how. I'm sure my father would love to tell you his theories about it. He'd do a better job of explaining it." She abruptly pushes herself back from the table and says, "I'm going to get a soda—do you want one?"

"Sure." She's ready to move on to homework, and I actually feel relieved. US History seems pretty tame after talking about a cosmic library of thoughts. I finish unzipping my backpack and pull out my textbook.

We keep the conversation light while we study. I'm enjoying helping her learn about the history of the United States, which she makes sure to point out is a mere couple hundred years old compared to the some European countries, which are over a thousand years old, and I remind her that the Native Americans were here long before this land became the United States. I also like just watching her and being near her. The silver bracelets she wears make a musical sound when she moves her hands to gesture or to push her dark, sleek hair back behind her ear. I like the way her smile lights up her face and makes the corners of her eyes crinkle. I can't tell exactly what color her eyes are. At first I thought they were green, but now they seem more hazel in the soft light from the chandelier. Eventually, it gets late and I have to go. I hoist my backpack onto my shoulder and get up from my chair.

"Thanks for having me over," I say. *Which is so lame.*

"I'll walk you out." I'm glad we don't have to say goodbye in the dining room or the front hall, where someone could interrupt us.

No one else is around when we go out the front door. Darkness has fallen and the air is cooler than during the day. We walk across the lawn, now wet with dew, to my van parked at the curb, and I stop at the passenger side door to toss my backpack into the open window. When I turn around, Renee is standing a few feet away, so I reach out to take her hands and pull her toward me. Now there's only a few inches between us.

"Thanks for having me over," I say again.

"You're welcome," she says, a smile lifting the corners of her mouth.

"Goodnight . . ." I lean down to kiss her. It starts off softly at first, just my lips touching hers, but when she lets go of my hands and puts her hands on my hips to pull me closer, the kiss deepens and becomes more intense. I encircle her with one arm and put my hand on the small of her back to pull her even closer. My other hand slides up her back to get tangled in her hair at the nape of her neck. Her lips part and her tongue darts into my mouth as she lightly traces my lips.

Our bodies are pressed closely together, and I feel a slow burning start to erupt in my chest. But I know I have to leave, so I regretfully release her and pull my head away to look down at her. Her lips are slightly parted, but it's her eyes that mesmerize me. It's like I can see into her soul, and I *know* her. Like she knows me. A recognition.

Out of the corner of my eye I see a flash in the night sky. I look up and see a shooting star blazing across the heavens. I quickly turn her in my arms and point.

"Look. Over there. A shooting star."

"Oh!" she says, and I know she's seen it. A brilliant trail of light streaks low across the horizon through the blue-black night in the eastern sky. I lean back against the van and wrap my arms around her waist to pull her toward me. Her head fits neatly under my chin.

"Did you know that the light we see from the stars is actually millions of years old because of the time it takes for it to travel across the universe? And they've just discovered a black hole that is eight hundred billion times the size of the sun. *Eight hundred billion* times bigger. It's hard to conceive."

"I like that you're the kind of person who takes time to look at the sky and wonder what it all means. Most of the time we're focused on small things, and miss the bigger picture."

"You mean there's more to life than what happens at Monroe High School?" I softly kiss the top of her head, and she turns around in the circle of my arms to face me. She rests her hands on my chest, and the tips of her fingers lightly trace the bare skin along the line of my collar bone. My skin feels electrified beneath her fingertips.

We kiss again and this time it's deeper and more passionate. I crush her to me and move my hands down her back along her spine, feeling its gentle curve into the small of her back. Renee makes a small noise and presses her body closer to mine. She pulls her mouth away and gently pushes her hands against my chest.

"I think I'd better go inside now," she says breathlessly. I'm glad she seems as affected by the kiss as I do.

"Yeah, I should go. I'll see you in class tomorrow. We have that field trip," I say, but I don't make any move to leave. I'm breathing heavily too. I brush a stray strand of her hair back from her face. Now, in the light of the moon, her eyes are an almost golden color, giving her a catlike appearance. "You have beautiful eyes. What color are they?"

"Thank you." She smiles and the crinkles appear again. "I guess you could call them hazel." She pushes away from me a little harder and I reluctantly let her go. She takes a step backward and then turns toward the house. "See you tomorrow." She gives me a little wave over her shoulder.

"Bye," I say and wave back. I watch her walk up to the house, admiring the way her hips sway gently back and forth, before I get back into the van. The drive home isn't long, but I might have floated the whole way for all that I was aware of it.

9

THE BUS HITS a pothole and throws me into the air. I land painfully on my tailbone on the unyielding pleather seat. Renee rebounds from her sharp connection with the seat and slumps against me. A nice side effect to the crappy shocks on the bus. I reach my arm around her and pull her in closer.

"Man, I can't believe they make the grade school kids ride in these things every day without seat belts. Highly hazardous," Cole says, deadpan. "I think one of my fillings is loose." He wiggles his jaw with his right hand. The fingers of his left hand are white from gripping the back of the seat in front of us. We've been riding in the bus for what seems like forever, and we're still about twenty minutes away from the Eagle River Coal Gasification plant. Will and Cole are in the seat in front of us, and they've turned around to talk to us. That is, Cole is talking to us. Will hasn't said much.

"So, Will, is your dad doing the 'tour guide' thing for us today since he's the plant foreman?" Cole asks in a neutral tone. He's trying to come off oh-so-innocent, but I know Cole, and he likes to stir things up. He goes straight for the soft underbelly just to see what will happen.

"You know what? I have no idea what my dad is doing, and I don't give a damn." Will turns to Cole and continues in a low, controlled voice. "But since you're so curious, I'll tell you. He moved out a week ago. Said he wanted to 'have a good time' and that he'd grown apart from my mom. Said 'these things happen.' He just walked out on us. He doesn't give a damn about us, so why should I give a damn about him?"

"Hey, man, I'm sorry," Cole says, visibly shaken from the force of Will's reply. He might even feel bad for provoking Will.

"Just shut the hell up for once, why don't you?" Will turns angrily to face the window, his back to Cole, effectively ending the conversation. Cole looks at us with a pained expression. Renee squeezes my hand.

I'm not sure what to do, but I reach over the seat in front of me and put my hand on Will's shoulder and say, "Dude, that sucks." Because I don't know what else to say. Will knocks my hand away and spits out, "Just leave me alone, will you?" so I guess that wasn't the right thing to do. I'm also pretty sure that now wouldn't be a good time to bring up seeing Will's dad with the younger woman. Maybe I can try talking to Will later one-on-one. Not that I'm looking forward to that conversation, but he is my best friend and all.

Mr. Ogle stands up in the front of the bus to give us last-minute instructions.

"Remember, class, we are guests of the Eagle River Power company while on this tour. Please be on your best behavior and *don't touch anything!* General questions are fine, but there is no need to try to advance your own environmental or political agenda by posing inflammatory questions or making any derogatory statements. We will have plenty of time for discussion on the ride home and in class tomorrow. Any deviation from this will be dealt with severely." A low murmur erupts from the students in response.

"Coal gasification does represent an improvement over traditional coal-fired power plants." Cole is directing his comments to me and Renee, since Will is still sitting with his back to us, his posture rigid, inviting no conversation. "But it still has issues."

"Right. Haven't we been going over this in class for the past two days?" I ask, annoyed. I'm not ready to let him off the hook for what happened with Will.

"Well, yes, we have." Cole is unperturbed. "But the whole process of trying to move away from burning fossil fuels to clean energy sources is really interesting from an economic standpoint. I mean, coal gasification does produce lower CO_2 emissions, but the fact remains that carbon dioxide contributes to global warming. And it's still pollution. The problem is that there is such a huge infrastructure of industry dedicated to coal mining, production, and burning. It's just easier to call coal gasification 'clean coal' than to focus on truly clean, renewable energy sources."

"What are you, like a spokesman for clean energy or something? You sound like a freaking commercial."

Renee hurriedly intervenes to head off an argument between us. "In some European countries, I think they are capturing the CO_2 emissions from coal gasification and pumping it into deep underground caverns, so no CO_2 is released into the atmosphere."

I take a deep breath to calm down. Sometimes Cole is just too much. "Yeah, I've heard about that. The problem is we don't really know what happens when we bury CO_2 emissions. Remember that village in Africa where the entire community was suffocated by CO_2 gas that escaped from underground into the air? It pushed out all the oxygen and the town suffocated before they even knew what was happening. We don't even know if the CO_2 pumped underground will stay there," I say emphatically. I'm trying to keep my voice dispassionate, but I find this all so frustrating. We should be focused on clean, renewable energy, not 'clean coal.'

Audrey, a girl sitting across the aisle from us, chimes in. "But the emissions from coal gasification are way cleaner than in regular coal plants. Less acid rain and smog, too. At least it's a step in the right direction."

"Yeah, wasn't that in the chapter we read last night?" I say sarcastically. Renee elbows me in the ribs. She's right, I don't need to be a jerk about this. I just don't get why we would settle for something that is almost right when there are other options that are totally right.

"What about coal mining? I mean, we've all seen the coal miners on TV who've been trapped in underground mines, and mountain-top mining has a really negative environmental impact," the girl sitting next to Audrey says.

"Yeah, that's totally true," Audrey says. "Just like the oil spill in the Gulf of Mexico and the one in Alaska back in the '80s. It's a huge price to pay for energy."

I can't really comment on the benefits of coal gasification, because it feels to me like that saying my Mamaw sometimes uses: "putting lipstick on a pig." It doesn't change the fact that it still creates pollution and global warming. So I look out the window at the passing corn and soybean fields. The cornstalks are standing over six feet high in the fields, waiting to be harvested. Every now and then there's a farm house surrounded with trees and the ubiquitous barn, sometimes red, more often white. Away from the city, on the flat farmland, the sky is an overarching dome, stretching from one horizon to the other. Today there are big, cottony cumulus clouds moving ponderously toward the east and rising like mountains high into the sky. In the seat in front of me, Will is glowering out the window, but I don't imagine he's appreciating the pastoral scene.

What does he think about his dad working at the Eagle River plant? The foreman position is pretty prestigious, and when Will's dad got the job, his family was really psyched about it. But what about now? Now that we've learned that "clean coal" is just a clever marketing name? And how is Will going to act around his dad while the class is at the plant? Even Mr. Ogle knows that Will's dad is the foreman.

In the distance, I see white smoke billowing into the sky. The smokestacks of the plant loom over the horizon above the cornfields. The white clouds spewing out of the stacks don't look much different than the innocuous clouds floating through the sky, but I know they are.

The school bus pulls into the parking lot of the plant and comes to a stop by the front entrance. Will still hasn't said anything since blowing up at Cole, and he has a thunderous look on his face. I just hope he can keep it together enough around his dad so he doesn't lose it again. I have an uneasy feeling about this, so when we all start filing off the bus, I let Cole and Renee go ahead and motion for Will to get in line in front of me. At first he doesn't get up, but then he just shrugs and moves into the aisle between me and Renee.

When we're all standing on the blazing hot asphalt parking lot, a woman with a clipboard and a high chirpy voice—not Will's dad, thankfully—calls us over to her and says that she will be our guide on the tour through the plant.

For the next hour we weave through the maze of the plant following the path of the coal gasification process. It's pretty interesting from an engineering and scientific standpoint, I guess, but I can't really concentrate. I've got this weird feeling of foreboding, and the longer we're in the plant, the more distracting it gets. I keep looking at Will and expecting his dad to appear at any minute, but Will is acting pretty cool, and his dad is nowhere in sight. Still, I feel like I need to stick close to him in case there's a confrontation or something.

Finally, we're back outside at the side of the plant where the trucks tip their loads of coal into the processing area. Our chirpy guide is saying, "There's a picnic area along the shore of the Eagle River where you will have your bag lunches, and Mr. Asplunth, the plant foreman, will come out while you're eating and answer any of your questions."

Shit. I look over at Will, whose face has hardened again. The prickly feeling intensifies and, instinctively, my muscles tense, ready. Miss Chirpy continues now with an even bigger smile on her face. "I understand that one of you is Will Asplunth, the foreman's son? Will, would you like to come inside and visit with your dad?" She looks at us happily, searching for Will.

All the students turn to look for Will as well. Standing beside me, he says through clenched teeth, "No, thanks. I'm going to eat on the bus." He turns abruptly and starts jogging across the unloading area toward the parking lot.

No! Stop! It explodes into my brain and before I can think I'm lunging toward Will and grabbing him by the arm, yanking him back toward me. I sense more than see, out of the corner of my eye, the dump truck coming fast around the corner, barreling toward us. I've pulled him so hard that his momentum brings him crashing into me and we hit the ground, scraping and bruising ourselves on the asphalt and landing in a tangle of arms and legs. The dump truck, going much slower now, makes a wide turn around our group and passes harmlessly by where Will and I lie on the ground.

"What the hell?" Will says angrily, shoving me away from him and clambering to his feet. "What was that for? I can't believe you actually threw me to the ground."

"That dump truck, I thought it was going to hit you," I stammer out. I *knew* it was going to hit him, and I just reacted. But it didn't even come close.

"What are you, like Superman or something?" he says sarcastically. "It was nowhere near me."

"I'm sorry. I thought it was. I guess I was wrong." I can't believe this. I was trying to save him from getting hit by a truck and I'm *apologizing*. I feel like a complete idiot. The entire class is staring at Will and me. He's glaring down at me, and I'm still on the ground, blood dripping onto the asphalt from where the skin is scraped off my arm.

Will takes a deep breath and lets out a whoosh of air. "It's cool man. Sorry for yelling at you." He extends his hand toward me to help me up. "Just don't pull that shit on me again, OK?" He gives a half-hearted laugh.

Mr. Ogle comes over to see if we're OK and find out what's going on. Then our guide takes the class over to the grassy area by the river for lunch and goes off in search of a first aid kit. I sit down in the shade under a tree, and Renee comes over to sit beside me. She puts her hand on my wrist below a spot on my arm where most of the skin is scraped off.

"Are you OK?" she asks, her eyes wide with concern. "What happened?" *What did just happen?* My goalkeeper instincts kicked in when I thought Will was in danger, but how did I know that?

The truck didn't come anywhere near him. I had an uneasy feeling all day, and then the sudden flash of *danger!* Had I been wrong?

"I don't know. I guess I thought the dump truck was going to hit Will, and I pulled him out of the way. I didn't think, I just reacted." I lean my head back against the tree.

"Why did you think it was going to hit him?" It's a reasonable question, but do I have a reasonable answer? If anyone would believe me, it would be Renee, so I decide to tell her the truth.

"It just flashed into my head when he started to jog across the parking lot. I didn't even see the truck at first. I just *knew* he was in danger." I shake my head and shrug. "But I guess I was wrong."

"Maybe," she says. "Or maybe you really did save him."

Just then, the tour guide arrives with first aid supplies and kneels next to me. "Here's some antibiotic ointment and bandages." And then to Mr. Ogle, who is standing nearby, she says, "I'm so sorry, but Mr. Asplunth had to take a very important phone call and won't be able to talk with everyone."

"Figures. Mr. Unreliable," says Will, who's sitting a few feet away, which surprises me since he was so actively wanting to avoid his dad earlier. I guess nothing his dad does at this point would be good in Will's eyes. I'm actually relieved that we won't be having any confrontations. I've had enough excitement for one day.

AT PRACTICE THAT afternoon, Will and I have to see the trainers to have our "injuries" checked out and to see if we're OK to practice. There is no way we're going to let a few scrapes and bruises stop us from practicing. We have a game on Friday, and we both want to be in the starting lineup, so we downplay how sore we are. I'm still in competition for the starting spot with Brett, and I don't want to give him any advantage. Even though it hurts like hell every time I make a save, I go through the whole practice anyway, through gritted teeth. That's what ibuprofen is for.

On the way home with Will, I figure this is as good a time as any to see if he wants to talk about his dad. He didn't say much during the rest of the field trip or on the bus ride home except to give me grief, along with everyone else, about throwing him to the ground. I just tried to blow it off and make a joke out of the whole thing.

After we get into Will's car and he turns on some music, he leans his head back in the seat, closes his eyes and lets out a sigh. "What a helluva day. I'm glad that's over."

"Yeah, me too. So things are pretty bad with your dad?" I venture.

"They're non-existent. He just took off. I haven't seen him except at the soccer game—not that he hasn't been calling and texting me. I just don't want to talk to him. My mom's a mess, and my little sister just keeps asking when he's coming home. I feel like I have to try to hold it together for everyone." He covers his face with his hands and pushes his fingers into his hair. "Whatever," he says, blowing air through his pursed lips, and then a moment later he says, "Dammit!" and pounds his hands on the steering wheel.

"I saw him in town about a week ago. He was coming out of a restaurant with someone—a younger woman. I didn't actually see anything, but it just felt off, not right, you know?"

"It's probably this woman he works with. He swears that he's not having an affair, but I bet he is. Why the hell didn't you tell me?" He turns on me accusingly.

"I don't know. I wasn't really even sure there was anything to tell. I didn't know what was going on with him at home."

"Yeah, well, next time you see something like that, tell me, will you?" he says angrily and slams the steering wheel again.

"Sure, no problem."

"You and Renee seem to be pretty tight these days. Is that helping you get in good with Dr. Auberge?" he says with an edge to his voice.

Now it's my turn to be pissed. "What the hell is that supposed to mean? Are you suggesting that I'm using Renee for the internship? That's pretty low."

"No." He leans back against the seat again and blows air through his mouth. "No, I know you're not using her. Sorry, man. My brain's rattled these days." He gives me a rueful smile. "Forget it."

I don't say anything because I'm still pretty hacked off. My hands are clenched in my lap, and I have to consciously relax my shoulders and flex my hands. People say shit like that when they're angry because there's a grain of truth to it. Part of Will must actually believe I would do that.

"Has Coach Swenson said anything to you and Brett about who's starting on Friday?" Maybe I'm just imagining it, since this is something we normally talk about, but his asking me now feels like another slam. I look to see if I can tell from his expression, but he's started the car and is looking over his shoulder to back out of the parking space. I decide to just let it go.

"Nope. We're both still hoping to start. He may wait until right before the game like last time, which is crap."

"You should be starting. You're better in the clutch than Brett. He gets rattled when the pressure is on, but that's when you're on fire."

"Thanks," I say, somewhat mollified. "Since Brett's a senior and he didn't start last year, I think Swenson is giving him an extra shot, which I guess in theory I support, but not so much when it involves me."

"Sitting on the bench sucks. At least playing is the reward for working our asses off in practice all week." He stops the car in front of my house. "*Adios, amigo.*"

"See you." I get out and slam the door shut. I feel sort of off kilter, like something isn't right with the universe. I'm so used to being pretty much in sync with Will—I mean, he's been my best friend since grade school—but lately, I don't know what to expect from him. This thing with his dad must be really messing him up.

I HADN'T PLANNED to say anything about what happened at the plant to my parents, but at dinner that night Marcie blew that idea for me.

"So, I heard you threw Will to the ground on the field trip to the coal plant today," she says smugly, taking a bite of food and chewing slowly while she watches for my reaction.

"Where'd you hear that?" I ask calmly. But I'm wondering how she could possibly know about it.

"The sister of one of the girls in my algebra class was on the field trip. She sent her a text." *Figures.*

"What happened?" asks my mom, alarmed. "Were you fighting?"

"No, it wasn't like that at all," I say, glaring at Marcie. "Will was just walking in the parking lot and I thought I saw a truck coming, so I pulled him out of the way. I just pulled him a little too hard and we both fell onto the pavement. It wasn't a big deal."

"Oh." My mom looks relieved. "Are you both OK then?"

"Yeah, we're fine. Just some scrapes from where we fell to the ground." I hold up my arms and show them the raw patches. "I don't know why Marcie even brought it up."

"Gross. Do you mind? I'm eating." Marcie makes a face.

"OK. That's enough. We don't need any bickering at the table," my mom says. She's big on having family dinners every night. I'm sure she read in one of her parenting books that it's important for kids to have family time at the dinner table, which I guess is true, but it's not like we're the Brady Bunch, or anything. "I'm glad both you're both OK. I'd hate to think what could have happened if you hadn't been there."

"Did Will's dad show you around?" my dad asks.

"No. He was going to come out and talk with us, but he was on an important call and couldn't get away."

"Hmm . . ."

"You mean he didn't even come out to see if Will was all right?" says my Mom.

"I guess the call was really important." I shrug. I wonder if they know anything about what's going on. It's not like they're friends with the Asplunths, but they do know them. I don't think they'd bring it up at the table with Marcie and Drew around.

"Thanks for dinner, Mom, I'm going upstairs to study." I grab my plate and glass and leave them on the counter for my dad to clean up. My parents aren't big traditionalists in most things, but my mom cooks and my dad does the dishes. I'm not sure he can even make anything more challenging than frozen pizza, which is what he makes when Mom's not home to cook. On my way out of the kitchen, I get four ibuprofen tablets. My shoulder is starting to throb.

I have a paper due on *A Farewell to Arms,* so I work on that for a while and then do some reading for my other classes. It was a rough day, and I'm beat, so I only last about an hour before I have to go to bed. I crawl under the comforter and am out almost instantly. In the dead of night I'm awakened by another nightmare, and this one's different. No violent explosion, but it's worse, because this time it's about Will.

It's a morphed version of what happened at the plant. What makes it a nightmare is that I know Will is in danger; I can see the truck running him down, but I can't move. I can't save him. His face is turned toward me, eyes wide with terror, but my legs feel like concrete, rooted to the ground. The really terrible thing, though, as if that's not terrible enough, is that I feel like I should be able to do something, like I know what to do, but I can't quite remember how. I watch helplessly as the truck careens toward Will and, just before the sickening impact, Will screams and I wake up.

10

I CAN'T HELP thinking about the nightmare when Will picks me up the next day for the remote viewing session with Dr. Auberge. I mean, it's probably normal to have dreams like that after something dramatic and really stressful happens. Isn't that what dreams are supposed to do? Help you sort things out? Still, it creeps me out to think of the look on Will's face with the truck bearing down on him. I glance over at him as we cross the parking lot to the physics lab. The evening light catches him from behind and shines through his blond hair, giving him a golden halo. Which is creepy in a way, too.

I'm brought out of my thoughts by Will asking me where we're meeting up with Renee.

"She said she'd be at the lab with Stephen."

"OK, that's cool," he says. "I can't stay the whole time. I've got a Spanish test tomorrow that I haven't studied for. So, are you guys going out now, or what?"

"We haven't really talked about it—it's only been a week. It's weird. You know how sometimes when you meet someone for the first time you feel a connection with them right away, like you already know them? That's how I feel with her. Like I've known her forever, and like I'm just getting to know her for the first time."

"Dude, that doesn't make any sense." We're at the door, and Will reaches to open it with one hand and pats me on the back with the other. "She's got you totally whipped already."

"Yeah, I guess." I don't try to explain. I'm not really sure why I even thought Will would understand. He just doesn't think about things that way.

We're supposed to meet Stephen and Renee in the office at the back of the lab. When we get there, he and Renee are sitting across from each other at the desk deep in conversation. Renee jumps up and comes over to us as we walk in the door. She kisses me on the cheek to say hello, which ignites a warm glow inside me that starts in my chest and radiates out, enveloping my entire body. I reach for her hand. I think in France people normally greet each other very warmly, so maybe this is just a typical hello, but I find myself feeling very happy about French customs.

"All right. Are you ready to do some more remote viewing?" Stephen stands up and rubs his hands together, which makes him look like a mad scientist plotting our demise. He isn't wearing a lab coat tonight, and his long, knobby arms stick out absurdly from his T-shirt. "Since you two seem to know each other," he looks at me and Renee, "why don't you take Eric to room B and I'll get Will started. It's the same set up as before. Fifteen slides, one minute to transmit, and one minute to record your impressions. Any questions?" We shake our heads. "OK, follow me."

Will and Stephen leave the room and take a right down the hall. I follow Renee to the rooms on the left of the corridor. Room B looks pretty much identical to the room I was in before. Desk, chair, computer monitor. I sit down in the chair while Renee turns on the monitor and logs onto the system. She's leaning across me, and I smell the lemon scent of her hair and feel the warmth of her body. I reach up and put my hand on her shoulder. She turns her head and smiles at me.

When she's done at the computer, it displays a blank, blue screen. "You're all set to go. I'll be back for you in half an hour."

The session goes pretty much the same as before. I watch the blue screen and try to focus on receiving images for the first minute, then input my impressions during the second minute. Like last time, it goes pretty fast, and I'm surprised when the last screen pops up saying SESSION COMPLETE.

When Renee comes in the room to get me, I'm stretching my arms over my head and moving my neck around to get out the kinks. I'm basically always sore. Another goalkeeper hazard.

"Want a shoulder massage? I'm particularly good at it," she says, putting her hands on my shoulders. Her touch is strong and firm. I can feel my muscles unknotting.

"That feels great. Your fingers are really strong." I'm actually surprised.

"It's from sculpting and throwing pots on the wheel. Wet clay is really heavy."

"I'd like to see your work sometime."

"I'd love to show you. I have some paintings that I'm working on at school that you can see, but I didn't bring any of my finished pottery over from France. It's too heavy and bulky. You can come by the art studio, though." She kneads my shoulders a minute more. "Enough massage for now. They'll be waiting for us." Reluctantly, I get up and follow her out.

Stephen and Will are already back in the office when we get there.

"I don't think I have time to do another session," Will says. "Stephen says he can tell us how we did, and then I've gotta go."

"OK, sure," I say, although I'd like to stay longer.

Stephen sits down at the desk with the computer and starts typing. After a minute, he sits back and says, "High scores again. You even improved a couple of percentage points." Then he looks up at Renee and me. "Are you two together, as in 'a couple'? Because if you are, we could do some more sessions with the two of you since we have the lab time."

I look at Renee, not sure how to respond to this. I'd like us to be a couple, but like I told Will, we haven't talked about it. It'd also be cool to do the remote viewing with her. She's looking at me with her eyebrows raised questioningly and a wicked little smile on her lips. I nod to her and smile back.

"Yes," she says confidently. *Gotta love that in a girl.* "We can stay."

"Great. I'm outta here," Will says.

Stephen leans back in his chair and puts his feet up on the desk. He motions for us to sit down in the two chairs on the other side. "I'd like to try something a little different. Eric is showing some good enhanced consciousness abilities, so I think we could do a more advanced type of remote viewing. It's basically the same idea of connecting consciousness at a distance, but in this case, Eric, you'll be trying to see in your mind's eye what Renee is seeing through her eyes. What's in the room around her. In the most successful sessions, the remote viewer can actually feel like they are in the room with their viewing partner."

"Sure. Sounds cool," I say, but I'm thinking about what Stephen said about me showing strong enhanced consciousness abilities. It makes me feel uncomfortable, self-conscious.

"OK, great. Wait here for a minute while I get Renee set up. We have moveable props in the subject room that we change out for each session." While they're gone, I wonder what it even means to have "enhanced consciousness" and look at the titles of the books on the shelves around the small office. There are a lot of beat-up science textbooks, mostly physics, but also some chemistry, biology, and astronomy and several mechanical and electrical engineering books. Mixed in randomly with the textbooks are novels and other books—Carl Sagan, Isaac Asimov, Carl Jung, David Bohm, and Ray Bradbury. Science fiction and science writers with a different perspective, maybe not what you would expect to see in a university lab.

Stephen takes me to the same room as before, but this time, instead of entering my observations into the computer, I'm supposed to say out loud what my impressions are, and the microphone in the computer will record me. Afterward, they'll analyze the recording to see how well I did. Stephen will also be able to hear what I say as we go along.

"Most people say they get the best impressions when they close their eyes and we dim the lights in the room. But don't get too comfortable. We don't want you to fall asleep. It's happened before," Stephen says. "The computer will make a pinging sound when the session begins. Ready?"

"Yes."

After he leaves I lean back in the chair, which, aside from the computer, is the nicest thing in the room. It's one of those high backed, padded executive office chairs. I close my eyes and wait for the ping. When it comes, I feel pretty odd talking out loud to myself and knowing that Stephen is listening, and maybe Dr. Auberge will listen to the recording later. But I ramble on anyway. I try to focus on Renee. Her face and hair and citrus scent. Her hazel/green eyes and musical bracelets. I try to imagine where she might be or what might be around her. I see her sitting in a cloth-covered chair, like a living room chair, and I can't tell if I am totally making it up or if I'm getting something. The colors on the backs of my eyelids are different shades of blue, from indigo to royal to pale powder blue. Then a field of blue. Little dots of blue. Now a yellow sun growing larger and exploding into smaller suns with flickering, pointed tongues of fire rippling all around them. I'm also getting random thoughts about things like having to mow the lawn and when my next paper is due in language arts and how my shoulder is aching, but I try to push them aside and focus my mind on Renee. Actually, it all seems pretty random. It's not like I can really picture anything for certain or tell the difference between my own chaotic thoughts and actual impressions I might be getting from Renee.

The computer pings again, announcing the end of the session. When Stephen comes to get me, I'm feeling pretty discouraged, but he's really hyped up.

"That was a great session!" he says, bursting through the door. Renee is behind him.

"Really? 'Cause I felt like I was just rambling incoherently about nonsense."

"Come with me." He grabs me by the wrist and drags me down the hall to what I presume is the room Renee was in. "Look." Stephen steps aside so I can go in first.

The room isn't large—about twelve feet by twelve feet, maybe. I step in and look around and then take a step back in surprise. In the center of the room is a table covered with a few objects, but in the corner is a blue, fabric-covered armchair and next to that a folding screen with a pattern of blue flowers running across it. Directly across from me, hanging on the wall, is a picture. It's a poster of Vincent Van Gogh's *Sunflowers*. Bright yellow sunflowers in a vase looking just like little suns surrounded by petals of fire. Blue chair, blue flowers, and bright yellow suns.

I take another step back—Stephen's looking at me like we won the lottery or something and Renee is smiling and happy, but I'm a little freaked out. I mean it's not like I actually saw Van Gogh's *Sunflowers* or the blue flowers on the screen in my head, but this is too close to be coincidence. Maybe there is something to this collective consciousness stuff, but I have no idea how I'm connecting with it.

11

RIDING THE BENCH really sucks. Before tonight's game, Coach Swenson pulled Brett and me aside and said it was Brett's turn to start and "show what he can do," so now I'm the one sitting on the bench watching the game. Which blows. The worst part may be that all my friends and family are here to watch me play, and instead I'm stuck on the bench. I'm rooting for us to win, and I want Brett to make saves, but I know that every time he stops a shot it's a point in his favor for being the permanent starter. I hate not being able to play.

The crowd erupts as Brett dives and saves a shot headed for the right corner. He gathers the ball to punt it downfield and directs the players where to go. I have to admit he's good. We're both good, but I'd like to think that I'm better.

His punt goes past the center line, and Paul intercepts it, settles the ball, and takes off toward the other goal. He doesn't have any help, but it doesn't matter because he's crazy fast and the other team is caught with only one defender in position in the backfield. Paul jukes around him and then it's just him and the keeper. The keeper comes out, but he's late and Paul chips the ball over his head and into the goal. Score!

Everyone on the bench is on their feet, yelling and pounding each other on the back. The crowd is going wild. I'm yelling along with everyone else, but I'm also thinking that it was Brett's punt that set up the goal. Good for Brett, not so good for me.

We end up winning the game two to one. In the locker room after the game, everyone is really pumped.

"Are you going to the party at Allison Fischer's house tonight?" Paul asks as he towel dries his hair. "It's gonna be awesome."

"Yup, I'll be there," replies Will. "Got to celebrate another win!"

"What about you, Horton? You going?" Paul asks me.

"Yeah, I guess." I've finished getting dressed, and now I'm shoving my gear and uniform into my bag. I probably won't even have to wash it since I didn't break a sweat. I don't really feel like I'm part of the win since I didn't play. Maybe going to the party will get me out of my foul mood. "Where does she live?"

"Out in that bird-name housing development on the east side of town. Avian Ridge or something," says Paul. "Just look for the cars."

Will and I leave the locker room together to meet up with Cole, Renee, and Bonnie, who are waiting for us by the field.

"Brett looked pretty good out there," I say, as we walk across the asphalt toward them.

"He made a few easy saves. Nothing spectacular, though," Will replies. "Don't worry, you're still the man." This makes me feel slightly better. "Did you see me rocking the defense? It's not all about you, you know."

"I saw you—you were a brick wall."

"You got that right. Nothing left for Brett to save anyway."

When we get up to where the group is standing, Will says, "There's a party at Allison Fischer's tonight. Bonnie and I are going. Cole, do you want to ride with us?"

"Affirmative. I call shotgun."

"No way are you getting shotgun," says Bonnie indignantly.

"Are you guys going?" she asks me and Renee.

"Do you want to?" I ask Renee.

"Sure, sounds like fun." She smiles at me as she smoothes her hair behind one ear.

"OK, we'll meet you guys there." I hoist my gym bag onto my shoulder.

The three of them leave, and Renee and I follow behind toward the parking lot. I have my head down literally and figuratively. Sensing my mood, Renee grabs my hand and asks, "Are you OK?"

"Yeah, I'm fine. It just sucks not to play." I do realize that having Renee waiting for me after the game eases the pain a bit, so I make an effort to lighten my mood for her benefit. "I'm starving. Do you mind if we grab something to eat before we go to the party?"

"Hamburger and fries again, American boy?" She pokes me in the side.

"No, burrito this time." We stop by my favorite fast food Mexican place that serves awesome burritos. By the time we get to the party, it's in full swing.

I have to park about a block away because of all the cars. We can hear the music all the way from the sidewalk outside the house.

"What will the party be like?" asks Renee.

"I don't really know. I don't go to many of these parties. I guess there'll be music and dancing and maybe food. Some people will be drinking and maybe smoking pot, but not everyone. That's really why I haven't gone to these much. I'm not into the party scene."

"Well, it could be fun. I love dancing." She links her arm through mine as we approach the door. "You know, drinking is different in Europe. Kids drink watered-down wine with meals from the time we're very young. It's not a big deal."

The door is ajar, so we go right in. A few people are in the entryway who I don't know. Pulsing light and music are coming from further down a hallway going toward the back of the house, so we make our way down the corridor toward the light. It's dark in the kitchen except for colored lights flashing and a strobe light pulsing from somewhere in the adjacent family room where people are dancing. I see Paul standing by the kitchen table eating Cheetos and drinking a Coke.

"Hey," I say when we get up to where he's standing.

"Hey, big guy! You made it." He claps me on the shoulder, hopefully with the hand that *isn't* covered with orange Cheetos cheesiness, and looks at Renee. "Introduce me to your friend, why don't you?"

"This is Renee." Paul wipes his hand on a napkin and then extends it to her. "And this is Paul—he's captain of the varsity team and a world-class striker."

"Nice to meet you," Renee says as she takes his hand and they shake. I'm impressed that she doesn't flinch away from possible Cheetos contamination.

"Very nice to meet you," Paul says. At least he didn't bow and kiss her hand like Cole.

"So what's going on?" I ask.

"I think Will and Bonnie are outside, and Cole is going crazy on the dance floor. What is with that guy? The girls love him." He shrugs. "The rest of the guys are all over the place. If you want something to drink, there's a cooler of soda by the back door. None of the hard stuff for you, dude, we're in training."

"Don't worry, I'm not into that," I say over my shoulder as I get drinks for Renee and me from the cooler.

"I see some people from my studio art class over there," Renee says when I hand her a drink. She points to a group of two girls and a guy on the other side of the kitchen. "I'm going over to say hello." I don't know any of them, but I think I've seen the girl with the long red hair before. She'd be hard to miss. The guy I've never seen before but I notice him right away. For some reason, I immediately don't like him. It's a gut reaction I can't explain.

"OK," I say, adding, "be careful," which I realize is an odd thing to say to someone who's just going across the room at a party. Renee gives me a funny look.

"I mean, have fun." She gives me a kiss on the cheek, and I take a sip of my drink so I can watch her over the rim of my can as she walks over to the group and greets them. The girls squeal and hug her and the guy puts his hand on her arm, which really bugs me, but I'm not sure if it's because he's giving me the creeps or because I'm jealous somehow, which would be weird, too.

"Nice," says Paul, pulling my attention away.

"Off limits," I reply. Not that I'm worried. It's *Paul* for chrissake.

"Yeah, yeah, yeah. You're just worried that she'll be overwhelmed by my Asian charm and good looks."

"Not what I was thinking, but if it makes you happy."

"So, actually, I'm glad you're here, because Will's been acting really uncool." Paul puts his drink down on the table and turns to me with a worried expression, a crease forming between his brows. "He brought a couple six-packs with him and he's been pounding beers all night. Bonnie's trying to get him to stop, but it's not working. I didn't even know he drank." He stops and runs a hand through his dark hair. "Maybe you can talk to him. Coach finds out he's drinking and he could be suspended or kicked off the team."

"OK, I'll try. He hasn't been too easy to deal with lately." I walk over and tell Renee that I'm going outside. She's laughing with her friends, and the guy is standing really close to her and leaning in to talk to her. This really gets me, but I ignore it. When I open the sliding glass doors leading onto the deck, a whoosh of warm air hits me, displacing the temperature-controlled air inside the house. Groups of people are standing around talking, and some people are smoking cigarettes. Will and Bonnie are in a corner by the railing with a group of Bonnie's friends and a couple of guys from the cross country team, the only other team that runs as much as soccer players. I make my way over to them.

"You made it!" Will says, and raises his beer can to toast me.

"Having fun?" I ask him, indicating the beer.

"Sure, just celebrating our undefeated status." He chugs a drink. "A little beer never hurt anyone. Everything in moderation. You want one?" He points to the mini cooler at his feet.

"No thanks. I don't want anything to jeopardize our winning streak—like being suspended for drinking. You know Coach Swenson doesn't make exceptions."

"Yeah, well how's he gonna find out? Relax, I already have a mom. Hey, but maybe you can be my dad." The others standing around us have been watching our exchange in silence and now they laugh nervously. Maybe it was a mistake to start right in with the drinking. I guess I don't get any points for subtlety. I meet Bonnie's eyes, and she gives me a pained look.

"Just be cool, OK?"

"I'm always cool. Cool is my middle name." He takes another swig from the can.

"Asplunth!" one of the football players from a group across the deck calls out. "I hear the soccer team is winning—hell yeah!" He holds up his own can as a salute. It's in a drink cozy, but I think it's safe to assume that it's beer, too.

"Yeah!" Will calls back. He raises his beer and says, "To winning!" Then he downs what's left in the can and gets another from the cooler. A small cheer goes up from the others gathered on the deck, and several of them toast each other with whatever they're drinking. Bonnie and I silently look at each other across the group.

I'm not celebrating mostly because I don't want to encourage Will, but also because once again I don't feel like I participated in tonight's win. I've never had to sit out before unless I was injured. It sucks, is all I can say. I stay outside and talk to the cross country guys for a few minutes and manage to get Bonnie aside and tell her to let me know if Will gets really out of control. Will essentially ignores me, so I go back inside. I want to see Renee, anyway.

Paul is still stationed at the food table watching the dancing, but now he's moved on to Chex Mix.

"Did you see what I mean about Will?" he asks.

"You're right, but he's not gonna listen to me or anyone else right now. I told Bonnie to come and get me if she needs help."

"We definitely need to look out for him. He's never acted like this before." Paul sounds really concerned, so I say, "He's dealing with some shit at home right now, so that could be part of it. I'll try to talk to him about it when he's not drinking." I look around for Renee, but she's not where she was when I went outside. "Have you seen Renee?"

"I think she's somewhere in the crowd dancing with Cole. At least that's where I saw her last."

I scan the throng of people gyrating in the darkened room. It's hard to see by only the light of the strobe, but I locate her dancing with a group of girls and Cole on the far side of the room, so I wend my way over to them, dodging bodies as I go. It figures once again that Cole would be surrounded by girls. I wonder if he realizes that they think of him as their safe guy friend and not in a boyfriend way. He does seem kind of asexual. Not hetero or gay. Not that it matters, but still . . .

I tap Renee on the shoulder and she turns to face me, still moving to the beat. I'm not the world's best dancer, but I can bust a move now and then, so I join in. The music's turned up loud and we can't hear to talk, so I just smile and watch her sway and turn, her dark hair swinging around her shoulders. The beat of the bass throbs rhythmically in time with the beating of my heart.

We stay at the party another hour or so, and I check on Will one more time before we leave. He's not acting too wasted, and Bonnie gives me a smile and a nod, so I figure I don't need to babysit.

I pull Cole out of the dancing crowd, where he's still holding court with all the girls whose boyfriends won't dance, to let him know that we're leaving. "Do you need a ride?" I ask him.

"No, I'll go with Will and Bonnie to keep an eye on the wild man and drive him home if I need to." He's breathing heavily and pushes his sweaty hair back from his face. "The pool's open all afternoon tomorrow if you want to come by."

"Sounds good. I may be over. And thanks." I indicate Will outside on the porch.

"Hey, I'm nothing if not loyal."

We can still hear the music as we walk across the lawn toward my van, but it's much quieter. The air is wonderfully warm, not oppressively hot like during the day. I reach for Renee's hand and pull her to me for a kiss.

"Do you need to get home right away? We could go to the lagoons for a while." I encircle her with my arms and hold her against me.

"Hmmm, I don't know. What do you have in mind exactly." She smiles up at me, arching her eyebrows.

"Oh, no, that's not what I meant, really. It's just a cool place to hang out, and maybe, you know, make out, but that's it, I promise. I'm not like that." I've never had a girl be so candid with me before. It's pretty cool not to have to guess about what she's thinking. Or to have those expectations put on me. I really like Renee and I think she's totally hot, but I think all those sex-ed classes must have had some effect on me. I've definitely had my share of experiences, but never all the way. It just hasn't seemed right. There's this idea that all guys want is to get in a girl's pants, which is probably true for some guys, but not for me.

"Then I would love to go with you to the lagoons. I guess I'm just a little cautious. Some of the American boys I've met think that because I'm French I drink red wine all day, wear sexy lingerie, and am always ready to jump in the sack. I'm sorry. I'm glad you're not like that." She squeezes me around the waist.

"You mean you don't wear sexy lingerie?" I say and pretend to peek down her shirt.

"That's my secret—for now." She laughs and pushes me away.

That gives *me* something to think about as we climb into the van and I pull away from the curb, but I'm also wondering about what other American boys she's talking about. Is she seeing other guys, too? It gives me a queasy feeling in the pit of my stomach.

"So, what are the lagoons?" Renee asks, breaking into my thoughts.

"A long time ago it was a big marshy area that the Indians called the Chewab Skokie, which means 'big wet prairie.' Back in the 1930s, the Forest Preserve bought it and made it into a nature preserve with lakes and waterways. Now people use it for hiking and stuff. I like to go running here." I pull into the parking lot and there are several other cars already there, scattered at a good distance from each other—probably couples like us with the same idea of being alone.

"Come on, I want to show you something." I open my door and motion for Renee to get out, and I take her hand when she comes around to my side. Cones of white light fall from the street lights above, creating regular rows of bright circles on the asphalt. I lead Renee toward a path in the woods that runs parallel to the road. As we pass through one of the circles of light, it suddenly goes dark. Not that I'm surprised. Practically every time I come here one of the lights goes out when I go under it.

"Oh!" Renee exclaims and looks up at the now darkened light. "It happened again. That is really odd."

"This is one of the places where it happens a lot."

"I wonder why? Is there something special about this place?"

"You'll see."

The half moon is partially risen, but its light doesn't penetrate the leafy branches overhead, so the woods are dark. We hold hands as we walk along the path not talking, just enjoying the velvety grey shadows and the quiet of the sleeping forest. As we round the last bend, I watch Renee to see her reaction to the scene before us. Her eyes widen and her mouth forms an O. She looks at me and smiles. "*C'est magnifique.*"

I can't help but smile back. I'd really hoped she'd appreciate it as much as I do. We step beyond the edge of the trees, and before us is one of the larger lagoons, completely encircled by woods. Moonlight shines down on the calm surface of the water, making it shimmer. But it's the massive boulder jutting out of the otherwise prairie-flat shore of the lagoon, rising twenty feet into the air, that's so arresting.

"Isn't it cool?" I ask. "It was left behind when the glaciers receded. Let's climb to the top—it's fairly level and we can sit up there." Over the years hundreds, maybe thousands, of kids have made a sort of stairway up the sloping side of the rock. I go first to show the way and help Renee clamber up behind me. At the top we stop to catch our breath. Renee looks out over the water and says, "I'd like to come back here during the day to paint. I bet the colors are wonderful. And now, at night, it's magical."

"My mom says the rock is on one of the earth's energy lines, or ley lines. Some people think all of the ancient sites like Stonehenge and the pyramids in Egypt are aligned together on the ley lines so the ancient people could access higher sources of energy."

"Really? That almost sounds like a way to tap into the Universal Energy Field."

"You're right, it does." I pause to consider this. "My sister Marcie calls it the 'star-watching rock,' like the one in those *Wrinkle In Time* books, where the stars sing to each other. I guess that's sort of like communicating through the Collective Unconscious." Renee sits down on the rock and pulls me down next to her.

"Do you believe we can really communicate with our thoughts?" I ask her.

She leans back on her elbows and turns to me. "Yes, I do. I think it's something we can learn. I know I have good intuition and I'm good at listening to my gut feelings, but I'd like to be better at it."

"Maybe we can work on it together." I lean forward to kiss her. She puts her hand on the back of my neck to pull me closer. The top of the rock isn't the most comfortable place to make out, but I'll take what I can get. I pull away and rest my forehead against hers. "Remember the other day when Stephen asked if we were a couple? Well, I was wondering what you thought about that. I mean, would you like to be a couple?" The question stumbles out. I feel like we're a couple, but I want to be sure about how she feels. Her breath flows gently against my chin as she breathes in and out. It seems to take a long time for her to answer, but then, to my relief, she says, "Yes, I would like that very much," and kisses me again.

12

I USUALLY TRY to avoid going to school on Saturdays, but Renee is working in the art studio and she asked me if I wanted to come by and see her paintings. I've never been to any of the art rooms, so I'm not exactly sure where the painting studio is and Renee couldn't give me very good instructions. I guess I'll figure it out.

I've got my tunes on random shuffle, and when I pull into the parking lot, "Strawberry Swing" by Coldplay is playing, adding to my already good mood. I crank it up and listen in the car until the song is over.

The door to the art department is propped open with a piece of wood, just like Renee said it would be, so I slip inside. The hallway is crowded with pieces of wood and paintings and rolling shelves filled with ceramic pots lining the walls. Artwork in progress. Dabs of paint or clay and a fine, chalky dust cover most of the exposed surfaces. The first room I pass has a few people sitting at long tables drawing, but I don't see Renee. Music is coming from somewhere down the hallway, so I follow it. As I get closer, I realize the song is "Strawberry Fields" by the Beatles. *Another strawberry song? Another coincidence?*

Renee is on the far side of the room with her back to the large floor-to-ceiling windows, working on a big canvas on an easel in front of her. She doesn't see me right away, so I can watch her for a moment. I can't believe how lucky I am and how right it feels to be with her. The beginning of a relationship is always exciting, but there's usually an awkwardness or uncertainty while you're getting to know each other. I don't feel any of that with Renee. It feels easy, like we've already gotten through that stage.

She's concentrating on her painting and chewing on her lower lip as she tilts her head to one side. Her hair is different than she usually wears it, up in a loose pile on top of her head. She steps back from the painting like she wants to get a different perspective and then she sees me standing in the doorway.

"Bonjour!" She calls out and puts the brush she's using in a cup on the table next to her. She wipes her hands on the smock she's wearing and beckons for me to come over. "I'm so glad you came. I want to show you what I'm working on."

I walk over to her and she kisses me on the cheek. I get a faint whiff of her perfume mixed in with the smell of turpentine and wet paint.

"It's not finished yet, so you have to imagine a little bit."

I turn to look at the painting and at first it just looks like a lot of color splotches and shapes on the canvas. *Maybe flowers?* I don't have any artistic talent and probably not much of an eye for art either, so I'm a little nervous about this. "It's very colorful," I venture. "What is it?"

She gives me a gentle shove. "Silly, you're not supposed to ask an artist that. It's an impressionist painting of my mother's garden at our house in France. It's for a school project, but I'm also doing it as a gift for her since she had to leave her garden behind." She shows me some photographs spread out on the table. "See, here are the flowers and the tomatoes and beans." I pick up the photos and look at them and then at the painting. Now I can see that the bright blobs of purple and yellow are flowers, and the red splotches are tomatoes. "What are these?" I ask, pointing to clusters of small red triangles near the bottom of the painting.

"Strawberries," she answers.

"Really? That's weird." I put the pictures back down on the table.

"What do you mean? Why are my strawberries weird?" She looks puzzled and slightly hurt.

"No, your painting is beautiful. It's just that driving over here 'Strawberry Swing' was playing on my iPhone, and when I came into the studio 'Strawberry Fields' by the Beatles was playing. A weird coincidence."

"Oh, I don't believe in coincidences." She picks up a tube of green paint and replaces its cap.

"You don't?"

"No. I think things happen for a reason. Maybe the universe was telling you something."

"About strawberries?"

"No." She replaces the caps of the purple and yellow paint tubes and says slowly, almost shyly, "About us."

"I like that idea." I put my arm around her waist. "That the universe is on our side. I really like your painting, too. Your mom will love it."

"Thank you. Careful, I'm covered in paint." She pulls away from me. "Here, I'll show you some other things that I've already finished." She unzips a large, rectangular portfolio case and pulls out some drawings and paintings. She's very animated, and I can tell this is what turns her on. Some of the drawings are of people, and some are scenery, and even I can see that she's really good. "These are great. You're very talented."

"*Merci.* I love doing it, too."

"So, what about taking a break now and coming with me to Cole's pool?"

"You go. I really need to stay here and finish this painting for class on Monday. It's easier here than at home—not so many distractions. The light's better here, too."

"OK, I'll be there all afternoon. Text me if you finish and want to come over."

IT DOESN'T GET much better than hanging out at Cole's pool. I'm floating on a raft, dozing in the sun, with my cold drink conveniently placed in the on-board drink holder. Cole just dove off the diving board and is doing a few laps. I get enough exercise during the week. Weekends are for chilling.

"You boys want some lunch?" Rhoda, Cole's mom, calls from the back porch. She keeps us plentifully supplied with munchies from her well-stocked pantry, or, as we call it, "The Mother-lode."

"What's on the menu?" Cole's stopped at the end of the pool, stretching against the wall.

"I could do pizza or corndogs or turkey sandwiches," she replies through the screened door.

"I vote corndogs!" I call out while keeping my eyes closed and my supine position on the raft. "Thanks, Mrs. Rosenberg."

"Yeah, corndogs sound good."

"OK. They'll be ready in about fifteen minutes. Are you boys wearing sunscreen?"

"Yes, mom. You can go now," Cole says in an exasperated tone.

My raft has floated down to where Cole is still stretching. "So how'd last night end up?" I ask quietly. Mrs. R has acute hearing.

"Not bad. We stayed another hour or so. Will had run out of beer by that time, and Bonnie was driving, so we didn't have that to worry about. He wasn't acting totally stupid."

"That's cool. He's never wanted to hang out and party with that crowd before. I think it's still pretty rough for him at home." I take a sip of my drink and shade my eyes from the sun to look at Cole.

"Who knows what makes Mr. Asplunth do what he does. He seems to be keeping it under control, though."

"I guess," I reply, but I'm not convinced.

Will arrives while we're eating our corndogs at the table by the side of the pool. True to form, Mrs. R has made enough to feed the entire soccer team, if by chance they should drop by, so there's plenty for him, too.

"Gotta love your mom, Cole. This is awesome," Will says, as he loads up a plate with chips and a banana and several dogs and pulls out a chair to join us.

"She has to stay true to our Jewish cultural heritage by plying us with food, although I'm pretty sure these corndogs aren't kosher," Cole replies.

"Well, I'm happy to be the benefactor of her hospitality," Will says.

"You are very welcome, William," Mrs. R says as she comes down the steps from the porch. I'm pretty sure she's checking to see if we are stuffing ourselves properly. "Just let me know if you boys need anything else."

We talk about music and school and nothing in particular while we're eating, and I can't help but notice that Will is especially jazzed up, almost hyperpositive. It seems forced. I feel like I should talk to him about the drinking, but I'm not sure how to bring it up without pissing him off. Like last night.

"How're things at home? How's your mom?" I ask instead.

"Not great. Dad's got an apartment now and my mom's like a walking zombie. I mean she's there, but she isn't really *there,* you know?" He taps his head. "At least she's not constantly crying anymore."

"That sucks," I say, knowing it's totally inadequate. "Is there anything we can do to help? Like meals or anything?" Isn't that what people always do in a crisis? Bring food? Not that I would cook anything, but I'm sure my mom would.

"Thanks, but my mom's friends have been coming by and helping us with stuff like that. We're all taken care of so my dad can go out and party, because isn't that what it's all about?" he says and tips his drink can toward me in a toast.

"Yeah, about that," I say slowly, figuring this is as good an opening as I'm going to get. "What's with the drinking? You know it could get you kicked off the team." Not exactly confrontational, but I see Will stiffen. Cole continues to eat his potato chips, wisely staying silent.

"Like I said last night, Coach isn't going to find out. It's not a big deal anyway, so lay off." He pushes himself back from the table, his chair scraping against the stone patio.

I figure I've done what I can by bringing it up and pushing harder won't get a better result, so I change the subject. "Renee told me that her dad's decided how he's going to choose the student for the internship. It'll be based on class grade, a short essay, and an interview."

"So when were you planning on sharing this information with us, huh?" Will asks sarcastically.

"What the hell? I'm telling you now. She just told me about it yesterday, and I think Dr. Ogle is going to say something to the class on Monday." I know Will's dealing with a lot of stuff, but that doesn't mean he has to act like a jerk. "Everyone in class has the same shot at the internship. Chill out."

"Yeah, whatever. I'm going for a swim." In one fluid movement he gets up from his chair, takes three steps to the pool, and dives in. He swims underwater to the far end and then turns and starts doing the crawl with long powerful strokes. Cole and I just look at each other. "That went well," I say.

"He's pretty touchy these days, that's for sure. Maybe we should back off a little bit."

"There doesn't seem to be much else we can do."

After we clean up the plates and bring the remaining food inside, Cole suggests we play three-man water polo, where we each have a goal to defend. Our games can get pretty rugged since we're all so competitive, and today Will and I are especially ruthless. But it's a good way to work out our anger and frustration. On the first play of the game, he slams the ball at my head to take me out and then scores when the ball ricochets off me back to him and he knocks it into my goal.

"I see how we're playing it," I say, but I'm laughing. "You'd better watch your back, Asplunth."

"Bring it!" he says.

On the tip-off I retaliate by shoving him underwater and grabbing the ball from Cole. I take off toward Will's goal, holding the ball in one arm and swimming with the other, and am about to send the ball in when I'm tackled from behind. I come up sputtering and see Will scoring on Cole.

"Gooaaal!" Will calls out, falling backward into the water with a splash.

"Maybe you should be playing striker," I say.

"Then who would be there to protect you from getting scored on?" he replies.

"OK, that's it, you've been warned. It's all-out war now!"

The rest of the game goes pretty much the same, with all of us alternately dunking and slamming each other to get the ball. Will wins by getting to twenty first, and we drag ourselves out of the pool and flop onto the deck chairs breathing heavily.

"That was awesome," I say, and hold out my hand to fist bump Will and then Cole.

"Nothing like a little full-out water polo," Cole says as he towels himself dry.

I laugh, but he's right. The tenseness between Will and me is gone. Will even brings up the internship again.

"Do you know where the internship's going to be? With the Universal Energy experiments or doing that mind-reading stuff?" he asks.

I wince, but I don't think he's being sarcastic. He's just not into the remote viewing. "No, Renee and I really haven't talked about it. Maybe we'll find out more from Mr. Ogle on Monday. Are you applying, Cole?"

"No, AP Enviro is cool, but science isn't really my thing. I just took it for the AP credits. You guys can duke it out." Which is exactly what I'm worried about.

13

I KICK ASIDE a pile of clothes on the floor of my room to see if the shirt I'm looking for is underneath it. Nope. It's possible that it got shoved under the bed, so I get down on my knees to look. There it is—a gray/blue Henley surrounded by several of Ralph's chew toys that he's "buried" under my bed. I pull it out and give it a sniff. Not too fresh. So it's time for the Eric "special" clothes wash. I grab a few more shirts that look excessively wrinkled and are not exactly smelly, but not exactly clean either, throw them in a laundry basket, and take the stairs two at a time on my way to the laundry room.

My special wash is a true time saver and last minute personal care miracle. I'm supposed to be doing my own laundry, but as it doesn't always get done, I devised this simple fix. A few squirts of clothes freshener on the item to be cleaned, then five to ten minutes in the dryer, and—voila!—clean, wrinkle-free clothes! The freshener comes in Spring Rain and Ocean Breeze scents. I prefer Ocean Breeze myself.

Marcie comes into the laundry room with her hamper while I'm spraying my shirts. She has to do her own laundry too, and as she is a little more fastidious than I am, she doesn't ascribe to the special wash method.

"Thanks for just dumping my clothes on the floor," she says. Her load had been in the dryer—finished, I might add—so I had to take them out to put my clothes in.

"Sorry, I have to do a load. Anyway, folding your clothes is not part of my laundry duties."

She starts pulling her clothes out from the pile, folding them and putting them into her hamper. She notices that I'm spraying my shirts. "Oh, the Eric special wash. Do you have a date or something? Are you dating that Italian girl who's always waiting for you after the games?"

"She's actually French, and yeah, we're dating. After dinner we're going to the Benton County Wind Farm. I want to take Dad's telescope so we can go stargazing too, at McCloud Park."

"We haven't been out with the telescope in forever."

"It's not your usual sort of date. I hope Renee likes it."

"She probably will. Most girls would think it's romantic." She's quiet for a minute, lays a folded red shirt on top of her growing pile and then says, "Do you ever think about star people? I mean, like if they exist or if they're actually already here, on earth?" This is not as weird a question as it seems. In my family we've talked about stuff like this around the dinner table for years.

"I think it's naïve to believe we're the only inhabited planet in the universe. But I have no idea about aliens. I guess they could be here, but wouldn't we know?"

"I think they'd be so advanced they could be hiding in plain sight. And maybe some people do know. Maybe the whole planet isn't ready to know about them and they're helping us without interfering." She's stopped folding laundry and is just looking at me. Now it is getting a little weird.

116

"Well, yeah, I guess, but who knows?" And then I just can't resist adding, "It almost sounds like you've got some inside knowledge, *Lieutenant Uhuru*. Beam me up, Scotty?"

"Very funny. Like that would ever happen." She starts swatting me with the shirt she's holding. "My mistake for trying to have a serious conversation with *you.*"

I hold up my arms to shield my head. "I'm sorry, but there was no way I could let that opportunity go by."

She stops hitting me and gets back to folding her clothes. "Didn't you go on a field trip to the wind farm last week?"

"My AP Enviro class went, but it's awesome to see at night. There's an amateur astronomer's stargaze tonight and I don't have a game, so I thought we could do both."

"That'll be cool. So, the soccer team's on a pretty good winning streak, right? What have you won now, like ten straight games?"

"The team's won thirteen, but I've only played in seven games. I'm splitting games with Brett Morgan. But it's still pretty cool. How's cross country going? Sorry I can't make it to any meets, you know, with practice and all." I'm done spraying the shirts, so I load them into the dryer and put the timer on for ten minutes.

"It's good. I'm really better at the middle distances—two hundred and four hundred meters, but I do OK in the longer races. I've had two personal best times the last two meets. At least I'm improving."

"That's cool. Hey, I gotta go. I need to find Dad and ask about the telescope."

I find him on the porch lying on the couch. The ceiling fan is revolving at high speed, fluttering the pages of the book he's reading. The breeze coming through the screens is just pleasantly warm, and the nights have been cool. There's a hint of that sweet rotting smell you get when the plants in the garden are past their prime and beginning to fade and wither.

"Hey, Dad, would it be OK if I took the telescope out tonight? Renee and I are going to the wind farm and I want to show her some stuff with the telescope." He puts the book down on the coffee table and looks over at me standing in the doorway to the house.

"Sure thing. Do you know what's in the sky right now? We could look it up before dinner if you want."

"I looked at Indiana Amateur Astronomer's website, and it says that M13 is visible, and so are the Ring Nebula and Saturn Nebula. I'm pretty sure I can find them. It's also the night of the Harvest Moon, so that'll be cool to look at, even though it'll make it harder to see the stars. Here, I printed off some stuff." I put the pages I printed from the site down on the table. He sits up and pats the faded cushions next to him.

"Have a seat," he says. "Maybe you can see the Milky Way. You know there are more stars in the universe than there are grains of sand on all the beaches on earth?"

"Yeah, I know." He's only told me about as many times as there are grains of sand in Florida.

"Dad, have you ever heard anything about the Universal Energy Field? Renee's dad is studying it."

"Oh, yes." He takes his glasses off and puts them on the table. "It's also called Dark Energy. Not because it's malevolent, but because we can't detect it. At least not yet. But we know it's there because of movements and behaviors of celestial bodies that can only be explained by the presence of an energy we can't directly detect." He taps his fingers on the pages spread out on the table. "So Dr. Auberge is studying The Field. Interesting."

"Really, you've heard of it? What is it?" My dad's always been an amateur astronomer, so he's into this stuff, but I'm a little surprised that he knows about the Universal Field.

"Dark Energy is some kind of cosmos-filling field of energy. It's everywhere in the universe. In fact, Dark Energy and Dark Matter make up almost 95 percent of the entire universe. The matter and energy we can see and measure are only 5 percent of the universe."

"That's crazy. That we really know so little about the universe."

"I think it can be overwhelming for some people, but I like to think of it as endless possibilities in an elegant universe. The hand of God is everywhere."

"You mean like 'God the Creator of the universe?'" We've gone to church sporadically my whole life, but I've never felt much of a connection with the God in flowing robes carrying a scepter directing events from his throne in the sky. Somehow, God seems both more personal and more unfathomable to me.

"I can't claim to really understand what God is, but I feel like God is a part of us and everything else in the universe," my dad says. "The Chinese call it 'Chi.' The energy or life source of all things. Does that make sense?" As with so many things, my parents have never really forced their opinions on me, but have allowed me to find my own way.

"Yeah, it makes total sense." I say.

TONIGHT I'M DRIVING my Dad's Audi, which is an improvement over the minivan, but not by much, as it's about a thousand years old. Still, it is a German-made sedan. Renee and I have the windows down and I've got some low-key driving music playing. Instead of taking the highway north to the wind farm, I decided to go the scenic route on the back roads. We pass through tiny one-stop towns with only a gas station and a quick mart and sometimes a flea market, and I wonder who lives there and what they do to make a living or for fun. It's at least half an hour to get to the nearest drugstore, let alone a movie theater or restaurant.

On either side of the road are fields of dry cornstalks with ears of corn still attached, like the kind people put by their doors to decorate for Halloween, and soybean fields turning from green to gold. Some of the trees are starting to turn orange and red, and goldenrod grows in swathes along the side of the road.

"The fields and sky are really beautiful here," Renee says, interrupting my thoughts. "The sky is so huge, like an enormous blue dome, and the clouds are amazing to watch."

"There isn't much to block your view, that's for sure. It's pretty flat up here, not hilly like in the southern part of the state. But you're right, it is beautiful." A flock of birds flies overhead, looking like a swiftly moving grey cloud. Several minutes pass as the birds flow by in a continuous stream. There must be thousands of birds moving together, migrating south. "It's too bad, what they said on the field trip, about the wind turbines interfering with bird migrations. I guess there's always a downside, even with something good."

"Yes, but I think interfering with bird migrations and some ground vibrations are pretty minor drawbacks when you compare it to the pollution created by burning coal and oil. That probably kills more birds anyway," Renee says indignantly. I'm preaching to the choir here.

We round a bend in the road, and the wind turbines rise up from the farmland before us. There are dozens of them spaced out evenly across the fields—enormous white sentinels soaring into the sky. Somehow they always seem alien to me, like they are visitors from another planet or giant transmitters sending messages into space. Each tower is topped by three curved blades, like a child's whirligig, and they appear to be moving slowly in circles when, in fact, they are whizzing around at 80 to 120 miles an hour. They move in a sort of choreographed dance. I don't get why some people consider them eyesores. To me they seem majestic and almost awe-inspiring.

I pull over into a small park with a playground in an unnamed town on the country road. We sit side by side on the top of a wooden picnic table to one side of the swing set. Renee rests her hand on my knee, and I pick it up and hold it between my hands. I have big hands—good for catching the ball—and her smaller hand disappears between mine. She smiles at me and tugs her hand free. I reach over to smooth her hair back from her forehead and then put my arm around her, pulling her close. She leans her head on my shoulder. The sun is just now setting, and we have a clear view of the western sky across the cornfields ablaze with color. We watch the sun go down and the sky change from pink and blue to orange and lavender and then dark blue and purple.

"It's really lovely—like an impressionist painting. Wonderful colors," Renee says. As night gradually replaces the day, lights on the top of the turbines begin to flash a warning to planes. Hundreds of red lights blink on and off in unison, appearing to be sending a message to more than just passing planes, reinforcing my feeling that they are communicating with some far-off galaxy.

"Somehow the wind mills mean more to me than just green energy. Having so many of them all together, spinning at the same speed and flashing in unison is so harmonious, almost cooperative." I feel so at ease with Renee, like old friends, that I can say stuff to her that I wouldn't talk about with anyone else.

"They're quite magnificent. Like gentle giants. Simple and elegant. We have wind turbines in Europe, but I've never seen so many of them together."

"Didn't they say on the field trip that it's the largest wind farm east of the Mississippi? It's good for the farmers, too. Extra money." I hop off the table and stretch out my back, leaning side to side. "I think it's dark enough to use the telescope now, but we have to get away from the flashing lights." I hold my hand out to Renee as she steps down from the table. "McCloud State Park is a little bit south of here on the way home. There's a good place there for stargazing."

The air is cooler now after the sun has set, and I put on my sweatshirt before getting back into the car. In the twilight we pass by more fields of corn and see fireflies hovering over the tops of the stalks, blinking on and off like little satellites. "I like the scenery of the Midwest," Renee says. "It's a more subtle beauty than the mountains or the ocean."

The drive into the park from the road winds through open fields of tall grass and fading wildflowers, illuminated now by the full moon that's risen in the east. I've come here before with my dad and the amateur astronomer's club. They have an area cleared on top of a hill with level spots to set up the telescopes. My dad's scope is a ten-inch Dobsonian, which weighs about fifty pounds. It's a good scope for an amateur. Easy to maneuver, but powerful enough to see space objects really clearly.

There are three other groups with telescopes already set up when we get to the top of the hill. I pick a spot off to the side and set up the Dobsonian.

"I've never done this before. What kinds of things are we going to look at? Galaxies and nebulas?" Renee seems excited.

"I thought we'd start by looking at the moon, since it's the Harvest Moon, and it's the closest thing to earth." The moon hangs in the eastern sky, a silver orb reflecting the light of the sun. I position the telescope toward it and focus on its surface.

"What's the Harvest Moon?"

"It just means the full moon closest to the Fall Equinox." I have a clear view of its pitted surface in the viewfinder. "Here, have a look."

Renee puts her eye on the viewfinder and a moment later exclaims, "Wow! It's so bright and so clear. I can see all the craters and everything," which is the reaction I was hoping for. After a moment she asks, "How big do you think the craters are?"

"A hundred miles or more across."

"It feels so close through the telescope. It's incredible to think that it's out there in space orbiting around us."

"I know, right? Let's look at some things that are much farther away." I locate M13 in the sky by its neighboring stars and focus the scope on it. "Here, this is M13, a globular star cluster." I move to the side so she can look.

"What am I looking for?" she asks. "I don't see anything except what looks like a faint white cotton ball. Is that it?" She sounds disappointed.

"Yeah, that's it. It's a star cluster of hundreds of thousands of stars, tens of thousands of light years away." I know this because I read up on it this afternoon in the stuff I printed off from the website. It's not like I've got it memorized or anything, but I wanted to appear like I knew what I was doing. "That's hundreds of thousands of stars like our sun in that one little puff of cotton. You have to remember that we're just using a ten-inch scope. The pictures you usually see of stars and galaxies are taken over a really long period of time. With much more powerful telescopes." I don't want her to be disappointed. I want her to feel the same awe I feel when I look at the stars.

"It's hard to get your mind around a concept like that. Hundreds of thousands of stars in that tiny spot in the sky." She's stepped back from the scope and is standing next to me looking upward. "You can see so many more stars here in the country. Even with the moon out."

"I'll tell you a story that will really blow your mind. A while back astronomers decided to focus the Hubble telescope on what they thought was empty space, to see what they would find. The first time, they focused it on a point in the sky the size of a grain of sand held at arm's length. They left it there ten days to gather light from that one spot. They found there were over three thousand galaxies each with hundreds of billions of stars in that one tiny spot. The next time they did it, they chose a different spot, and the technology was even better. They found ten thousand galaxies. The stars we see in our sky are all from our own galaxy, the Milky Way. There are over one hundred billion galaxies in the universe."

"That's absolutely incredible." Her face is lit from the moon above. "What's that reddish pulsating star over there?" Renee points to a spot in the southern sky just above the treetops.

"I think that's the red super-giant star Antares." I pull out the map of the sky I printed from the website and look for it. "Let me get it into view." I move the scope to that section of sky.

We look at several more objects and check out what the other groups are looking at through their scopes before the chilly air makes us decide to call it a night. On the ride home we hold hands, but we're both quiet, lost in our own thoughts.

I pull up in front of Renee's house, and we spend several enjoyable minutes kissing each other good night. I've pushed the driver's seat way back, and Renee's climbed over the gear shift and is sitting on my lap. She sucks my lower lip into her mouth and lightly bites me, sending shivers up my neck and making my hair practically stand on end. Then she leans away from me against the steering wheel.

"I don't think I've ever had such a wonderful date. Thank you for showing me the wind farm and taking me stargazing. You are so much more than you seem, American boy."

"In a good way, I hope."

"Oh, yes, in a very good way." She kisses the tip of my nose. "My dad wanted me to tell you to bring a personal item from a family member to your session this week. He wants to work with you alone on some more in-depth stuff."

"Just the two of us?" I can't help that my voice comes out a bit froggy. I mean, Dr. Auberge is pretty cool and all that, but he's still Renee's dad and it's not like we're best buds or anything. Mostly I've been doing remote viewing with Renee and Stephen and sometimes Will, but Will hasn't been all that committed to going.

"No, not just the two of you, I'm sure Stephen will be there too." She shakes her head at me. "I think he's been impressed by what you've done in the lab and wants to take it a step further." She presses her palms against my chest and splays out her fingers, resting them at the base of my throat. I can feel my pulse beating against the tips of her fingers.

"What does that mean, 'take it a step further?'" It has a slightly scary connotation to it. "He's not going to hook me up to a machine or something, is he? And then measure my brain waves?" I bring my face down to kiss her just below her ear where her jawline meets her throat. "Because that doesn't sound like fun to me."

"Mmmmm," she murmurs, leaning her head back. "Maybe some brain wave measuring, but it doesn't hurt or anything like that."

"OK, then. I'll do it."

"I need to go in now." She gives me one last kiss and then crawls back to the passenger seat and gets out of the car. I wait in the car until she gets the front door open. The porch light above her reflects off her hair, making it shine. She gives me a little wave before going inside.

14

"THE WINNING STREAK continues!" Will announces as he arrives at my locker during passing periods. We won again last night against Dublin Heights with Brett in the goal. "My mom just texted me that the state rankings came out, and we're number one!" He holds up his hand to high five me.

"Awesome," I say, smacking his hand. I'll take that even with Brett playing.

"And," he pauses for emphasis, "we're nationally ranked—number twelve in the country." Paul has just come up behind him to hear this piece of news.

"Only number twelve?!" he says in mock indignation. "We are totally number one!" He raises his hand to fist bump me, too.

"So the game on Saturday in Fort Benjamin is critical," Will continues. "It's our last game of the season before sectionals. We could have an undefeated season—and they're ranked number two in the state. It'll almost be like a championship game." He pokes his finger into my chest. "You'll be starting, big guy, so you've got to be on your game."

"Always," I say curtly. I don't think Will even notices. I'm trying to keep it light, but that really pisses me off. What happened to the old Will who always had my back? This new Will is into partying and hanging out with the "cool" crowd, who he never would have had time for before.

"Hey, man, Eric's the beast," Paul says. "Chill out."

"Yeah," Will says distractedly. He's looking down the hall at a group of guys coming our way.

"Asplunth!" one of them calls out when they see him.

"Hey!" he calls back. Turning to Paul and me, he says, "I'll catch up with you guys later." Then he joins the group of guys, who start pounding him on the back and saying, "Number one!" Will is smiling and laughing. I turn back to my locker to get my books.

"What is with him?" asks Paul. "He's all about the party crowd now. When did he start hanging out with them?"

I straighten up and shut my locker. "I don't know. I guess that night at Allison Fisher's party."

"I thought you guys were best friends, and he could so totally get busted and kicked off the team. No more 'Mr. Number One' then." He looks after Will, who's almost at the end of the hallway, then at me, and smacks me on the shoulder. "Don't sweat Saturday, dude. You are going to rock that goal. Nothing's gonna get past you."

RENEE SAID I should bring a personal item from someone in my family to the session with Stephen and her Dad, so I decided to bring one of Drew's stuffed animals. It's a llama that he sleeps with every night. He named it Bacon when he was about three because he loved bacon so much. He still loves bacon and has been known to eat the entire pound my Dad makes sometimes on Saturday mornings, if the rest of us don't get to it in time.

Drew was really excited to be included in my session with Dr. Auberge when I asked him if I could borrow Bacon. "What are you gonna do with him?" he asked.

"I'm not really sure. Maybe use it to see if I can spy on you from the lab."

"Really? Cool! Do you want to take Round, too?" Round is a stuffed horse. We never could figure out why he named it Round.

"Nope, I think Bacon will do it. I'll let you know how it goes in the morning."

So now Stephen and I are sitting in the lab office waiting for Dr. Auberge with Bacon on the desk between us.

"We've never used a stuffed llama before for the remote viewing," he says.

"I'm just keepin' it fresh for you," I reply. "It's my younger brother's, and he has a pretty strong connection to it. I thought that would help."

"That's great. Younger kids are really receptive to this stuff."

The door opens and Dr. Auberge comes in. I'm still kind of freaked out by him, being that he's Renee's dad and a famous physicist. And he's so intense. He takes the chair next to me in front of the desk and sets his briefcase on the floor. "Eric, tonight I'd like to stretch you a bit, if that's OK with you." He looks at me as if expecting me to answer, so I say, "Sure, that's OK," not really knowing what I'm agreeing to.

"You're showing some good abilities in your remote sessions with Renee and in your experiences when playing soccer—sensing how the play will go before it happens." He puts his hands on his knees and leans forward—fixing on me intently. "What I have in mind is really twofold. Did you bring the personal item from a family member?" I nod and point to Bacon.

"This is my little brother's."

"Splendid. We'll use it to facilitate the remote viewing. We've found that using personal items really helps in connecting to the other person—kind of like a bridge. First, we'll do a more advanced type of remote viewing. Then I want to conduct some experiments with the Universal Energy Field." He had picked up the stuffed animal and was holding it while he talked. Now he stands, puts Bacon back on the desk, and begins pacing. I tilt my chair back and hold on to the edge of the desk for balance. "As you know, I'm researching The Field as part of my work here. I'm also doing these remote viewing sessions to study the Collective Consciousness. You could call it my side project. The idea of the Universal Energy Field, or Dark Energy, is becoming more widely accepted in scientific circles, but the concept of the collective consciousness, of one source for the combined thought energies of humankind, is more difficult to grasp, as you can imagine. Even though it's been talked about by people like Freud and Carl Jung. My theory goes even further. I believe that these two fields are actually *one* field." He stops pacing and looks down at me. Stephen is looking at him in rapt attention.

"Wow," I say. Lame, but what do you say when someone lays an idea like that on you?

"My experiments with The Field involve using instruments to access the energy, and I've been having some success, but I believe that it's possible to access both the information and the energy in The Field with *our thoughts*. I think you may have the ability to do that."

"Me? How?" This is so unexpected that I lose my grip on the desk and almost tip over backward before my chair comes crashing to the floor.

"We'll talk more about that when we start the experiment. I think we've had enough talk and theory for now. Let's get started with the remote viewing session." He moves toward the door.

"Wait," I say uncertainly. "I have no idea how any of this works or what I'm supposed to do. Maybe you're wrong, and I can't really do it."

Dr. Auberge turns and sits back down in the chair beside me. "Eric, science is about exploring the unknown and experimenting with things until you make a discovery. The whole point is that we don't know how any of it works. That's what we're trying to find out." His dark eyes focus on me intently. "Whatever happens will be the right thing. Are you ready?"

I take a deep breath and nod. "Yes." Even though I'm not feeling ready at all.

I follow Stephen and Dr. Auberge down the corridor to one of the rooms, but what I really want to do is run like hell away from here. I mean, the sessions I've been doing with Renee have been fun and pretty cool, but this idea of accessing the energy field with my thoughts is something else altogether. What does that mean anyway? What if I can't do it?

What if I can?

They take me to one of the rooms I've been in before. This time, after I'm seated in the chair, Stephen affixes some electrodes to my scalp and flips on a microphone. I've got Bacon clutched on my lap.

"For this session, I want you to use your younger brother's toy to help you travel to where he is. To actually see him and be present in the space with him. You'll be using the energy from the toy to connect with him," Dr. Auberge says.

"How do I do that, exactly?" It's not like they've given me an instruction manual or anything.

"You can't do it intellectually, you have to *feel* it. Just relax and think about your younger brother—what is his name?"

"Drew."

"Reach out to Drew with your thoughts. Try to connect with him. Be focused, but not forced. Like when you're in the goal and when you have been connecting in the sessions with Renee. Open, receptive, ready."

Stephen says, "The electrodes will be recording your brain waves during the session, and we want you to describe what is happening out loud so the microphone can pick it up. The session will last up to one hour, depending on what's happening, so get comfortable. Are you ready?"

"Yeah, I guess."

They turn out the light as they leave, and I'm sitting in pitch blackness. *All right then, let's get to it.* I'm still not sure how exactly to go about this except for what worked with Renee. I try to get into the mind frame I use for games, centered and focused. I push my fingers into Bacon's fur and think about Drew. My little buddy. *Where are you? In your room?* I imagine Drew's room. His bookshelves full of fantasy books and his treasures—an alligator jaw, geodes, arrowheads—all neatly arranged. His bunk bed with the solar system comforter.

I feel like I'm looking down at the scene from somewhere up at the ceiling. The posters on the walls look so real, like I could reach out and touch them. I'm reaching out my hand when I hear Drew say, "Goodnight! You don't have to tuck me in." The door opens and Drew comes into the room. He's in his Spiderman pajamas ready for bed. Ralph trails behind him. After Ralph takes a few steps into the room, he pricks up his ears and looks up—right at me. Then he lets out a little woof. Like a greeting! Can he see me? Does he know I'm here? Drew turns around and sees Ralph looking up at where I am. He kneels down and puts his arms around Ralph's neck. "What is it?

Do you see something? Eric said he was going to spy on me. Maybe he's here."
He looks around the room. "Are you here Eric? I left you a message on my
top bunk." He gets up and moves toward the bed. Ralph jumps up and circles
into a nest at the foot of the bed. I float across the room to the bunk bed. On
the top bunk, there's something white on the blue comforter. I move closer. It's
a piece of paper. On it is written, "Hi, Eric!" and a drawing of a space ship.
Then the light goes off and I hear Drew say, "Goodnight, Eric."

I feel Bacon's fur beneath my fingers. I open my eyes and it's
pitch black, but I know I'm in the lab. "I'm back," I say.

I sit in the dark, hearing Drew's words echo in my head and
seeing the note he left for me. *Was it real? Did I somehow travel to
Drew's room?* The thing is, I'm not really sure, but I think maybe
I *did*. I mean, I heard Drew *talking to me* and it seemed like Ralph
was aware of me. Is that even possible? Why am I even asking
myself if it happened? Either I imagined it or it was *real*.

The door opens and the light comes on, momentarily blinding
me. Behind me, Dr. Auberge says, "Young man, it seems you
have done an astral projection. How do you feel?" He puts his
hand on my shoulder.

I think about that for a moment. "I feel OK. Pretty weirded
out, I guess. And energized. Like adrenaline is zinging through
my veins." I twist around in my chair to look at him. "Did that
really happen?" I ask, as if somehow he would know more than
I could.

"There are many accounts of people being able to do exactly
what you just did. People who've had near death experiences,
psychics, and spies doing remote viewing for governments, so
yes, I do believe what you saw was real. You'll be able to get
confirmation when you talk to your brother."

They give me a few minutes to take a break before we move
on to the Universal Energy Field experiments. In the bathroom, I

splash cold water on my face and look at myself in the mirror. It's a strange feeling to have done something I never even knew was possible. And I have no idea how I did it, or what it even is. *Astral projection?* Dr. Auberge didn't really give much of an explanation. It's not the kind of stuff that happens in real life, to real people. Right?

Then I think about Drew, and I know I saw him and heard him. It was real. I grip the sides of the sink and stare at my face in the mirror. I still look like my normal self. And if I'm honest with myself, the astral projection, or whatever it was, felt perfectly normal, too. But what was it? I'm pretty sure my body didn't leave the room, if I can be sure of anything, so did just my thoughts go to Drew's room? Or my spirit or soul? It's way too deep for me to figure out, so I decide not to try. I grab a paper towel from the dispenser, dry my face and hands, and open the door to find out what the two mad scientists have in store for me next.

Back in the lab, I follow Stephen to a section of rooms I've never been to before. He takes me to a door with a sign that says AUTHORIZATION REQUIRED FOR ENTRY in large black letters. Pulling a key from his lab coat pocket, he unlocks the door and pushes it open. The first thing I notice when we enter the room, before Stephen switches on the light, are all the glowing dials on the equipment and computer monitors set up on tables lining the walls. Then I hear the hum of machinery and intermittent beeping noises.

"This is where we're conducting experiments on measuring and harnessing the Universal Energy Field." Stephen gestures to the machines, which I can now see are organized into more than a dozen different experiments with data rapidly displaying across the screens of the computer monitors. "We're trying different methods for accessing the energy and have been able to power small machines for short periods of time. It's not like we're ready to light up New York City, but it will happen. The energy is there."

Dr. Auberge comes into the room behind us. "What we'd like you to do, Eric, is try to tap into the energy field with your thoughts." *Oh, is that all?* He leads me to one of the experiments. It has a black panel with a series of about thirty tiny light bulbs in a line from the top to the bottom next to some sort of meter. Stephen pulls over chairs for us to sit in. "Everything in the universe is essentially made up of particles of energy, even our thoughts. There is growing evidence that we can affect the world around us with our thought energy. I believe we do it by connecting with The Field."

"What do you mean 'affect the world around us?'" I'm imagining superheroes exploding buildings with mind power, but I don't think that's what he's getting at. "I mean, I'd like to help, but I really don't have any idea how to do this. I've had the occasional street light go off when I walk past, but it's not like I'm doing it on purpose or anything."

"Many studies by highly respected researchers show that we can control our environment with our thoughts. They measured examples of prayer having a positive impact on health outcomes, athletes improving athletic performance, monks being able to walk across hot coals without being burned, and so on. Einstein even called it 'spooky action at a distance.' It's not really new, we've just never connected it to The Field," says Dr. Auberge. "Since you're already showing some natural ability, perhaps you can learn how to consciously and intentionally tap into The Field with your thoughts. So tonight, I just want you to try and light up the light bulbs on this panel." He positions the panel in front of me. "The meter alongside the bulbs will measure the intensity of the energy corresponding to the bulb you've illuminated." This sounds simple enough, but I still don't get it.

"What am I doing that gets the bulbs to light up?"

"That's what we are here to determine. Basically, use your thoughts and imagination. Don't touch the panel with your hands. Instead, *think* about the meter moving, about the energy flowing, about the bulb lighting up. When you're doing it right, you'll know because you'll see the meter move and the bulb light up. Immediate feedback. You can start whenever you're ready."

This almost seems like a joke—*think about lighting up the bulbs?* Dr. Auberge and Stephen are taking it totally seriously, though, and I'm pretty sure that I did just travel to Drew's bedroom remotely. As Drew himself says: "Anything's possible." Keep in mind that he's only eight, but why couldn't something like this be possible? I think I finally get it, too. It's like visualizing myself making saves in the goal.

Stephen and Dr. Auberge are sitting on either side of me waiting expectantly for me to start, which is making me really self-conscious. "I think maybe it would work better if I try this by myself for a while, if that's OK."

"Of course," says Dr. Auberge. He stands and pushes back his chair. "Stephen and I will analyze the data from some of the other experiments at the workstation across the room. Let us know if anything happens." It's the first time that I've seen Dr. Auberge be anything except calm and professional. He seems almost excited.

I'm left just looking at the black panel with all the little lights. I decide to start at the bottom and work my way up. Seems as logical as any of this can be. I think, *Light up!* And, *Turn on!* And . . . nothing happens. I try imagining the meter moving up, registering some energy flow. I think about energy flowing from me to the light bulbs. I imagine the lights glowing and blinking and all sorts of other things, and . . . nothing. This goes on for about half an hour, and I'm starting to get really tired and frustrated, and I'm also thinking that this is really stupid. I'm about ready to give up, and I'm just looking at the lowest light bulb, not really thinking about how it will light up, just seeing it glowing in my imagination . . . and I think I see it flicker. The meter moved just a tiny bit. It didn't last very long, and I'm not positive it really happened. I try to get the same feeling again, and this time I'm sure the bulb glowed for just an instant.

I jump out of my chair. "Hey! Stephen, Dr. Auberge—I think I did it!" They come quickly over from where they have been working across the room. "The lowest bulb definitely flickered on for a moment."

"Really?" Dr. Auberge says. "Stephen, would you check the data records please?" Stephen is already standing at the computer terminal pulling up the data.

"Yes, there are definitely two small surges of energy here. You really did it!" He turns and gives me a big hug, which I wasn't really expecting, but what the hell! I'm pretty stoked, too, so I hug him back. When Stephen releases me, Dr. Auberge clasps my hand in both of his and shakes it vigorously.

"This is wonderful, Eric. Really wonderful. Do you think you can do it again, while we are observing?"

"I'll try." I sit back down facing the panel and focus on the light bulb. It takes a few minutes for me to capture the feeling I had before, and I'm more than a little nervous with the two of them watching, but eventually, the meter moves up a fraction and the light bulb briefly glows.

"Two successes in one evening. I couldn't be more pleased. I know you're probably tired and ready to go home, but perhaps you could practice for just a few minutes more until you really feel comfortable with how to do it? That way you won't have to relearn the technique for next time."

"No problem." I stay for another fifteen minutes and by the time I leave, I'm able to get the light to glow a little brighter and stay on a bit longer, but I'm not always able to do it. I'm still not totally sure *how* I'm doing it.

Driving home on the familiar streets of town past neighborhoods filled with people doing normal, everyday things makes it hard to reconcile what happened in the lab. I mean, I'm driving my mom's minivan—it doesn't get much more mundane than that. But then, things like smart phones and computers would have seemed like magic to people not that long ago. More than anything, it makes me wonder what other things could be out there in the world that we don't know about. What other abilities could we have that we've yet to discover?

It's late when I get home; only the light over the kitchen sink is still on downstairs. My parents are in their bedroom getting ready for bed, so I knock on their door and stick my head in to let them know I'm home. I'm about to go down the hall to my room, but as I pass Drew's room I stop. *Would the note be there?* I put my hand on the knob and for a moment I'm almost afraid to find out. Then I remember Drew in his Spiderman pajamas leaving me a note with a spaceship on it, and I realize there's nothing to be afraid of.

The knob makes a soft click when I turn it. Light from the hallway spills in a rectangle across the floor and onto Drew sleeping in bed. Ralph is still curled up at the foot of the bed. He lifts his head and thumps his tail when he sees me. I walk quietly over to the bed and stroke Ralph's head. Drew has both arms flung out to the sides. His chest rises and falls, and his breath whiffles slightly through his nose. Spidey stares back at me from the front of his pajama top. I step onto the wooden bedframe and hoist myself up so I can see the top bunk. The note is lying on the solar system comforter. Right on top of Saturn. I pick it up and see, in Drew's little boy writing, *"Hi, Eric!"* and the picture of the spaceship with a boy, probably Drew himself, blasting off into space.

15

DREW IS EATING cereal at the kitchen table when I come down in the morning. I get a glass of orange juice and a bowl and spoon and sit down next to him.

"Did it work?" he says excitedly. "Did you see my note?"

I pour cereal and milk into my bowl before I answer. "Yeah, I saw your note. Thanks, buddy. It really did work," I say quietly. For some reason I don't want my whole family to be in on it, to start analyzing and talking about it. Unfortunately, my mom walks in just then and Drew has other ideas.

"I knew it! Ralph saw you, didn't he? Did you hear me talk to you?" It's like a totally normal thing to him.

"What's so exciting? What did Ralph see?" Mom comes over to the table and ruffles Drew's hair with the hand not holding her coffee mug.

"Eric was doing experiments with Bacon last night and he came to my room! I left him a note on the top bunk and he saw it!"

"He did?" She looks at me with a little smile, as if to say, *Isn't Drew cute, let's humor him.*

"Yeah, I think I actually did," I say in a serious tone. The smile slowly fades from her face, replaced by a look of mild shock. "We were doing remote viewing experiments with a personal object, and I used Bacon. I saw the note Drew left me, and I'm pretty sure Ralph knew I was there." It feels weird to be even saying what happened out loud.

"Wow." She sits down at the table. I guess that's not what she expected me to say. "Really? You really did that?" She's sounding more incredulous now. I just nod and shrug. "How do you do something like that?"

"That's the thing, I don't really know exactly how I did it. It sort of just happened." I look at her out of the corner of my eye. She's sitting in the kitchen chair holding her coffee, and even though she looks a little stunned, she's not totally freaking out or anything. "So do you actually believe me? You don't seem completely shocked." Part of the reason I didn't want to talk about it is that I was pretty sure most people wouldn't believe me. It's like saying I was abducted by aliens or something.

"Remember that summer a couple years ago when Marcie got President Stoller to stop development of those homes in James Woods at the lake? And the next summer when we were doing the archaeological dig? She was having visions and premonitions about things that turned out to be very real. I'm also pretty sure that my grandmother was clairvoyant or had second sight, so it's not surprising to me that you would have it too."

"Well, it was pretty surprising to me."

"Do I have second sight, too?" Drew says very seriously.

"You could. Maybe we all do, honey." She finishes her coffee and checks the clock on the wall. "You'd better get your stuff together to catch the bus, Drew." He jumps down from the table and gets his backpack, giving Mom a hug on his way to the door. "Bye, Eric!" he calls as the door slams shut behind him.

"What about you?" I ask her.

"You mean, do I have premonitions or visions?" She sets down her coffee. "Well, I don't think I do a very good job of cultivating it. I'm too practical in many ways, but there have certainly been times when I've gotten feelings about you kids or your dad that I paid attention to that turned out to be true." She looks at me for a moment. "How do you feel about it?"

Of course, she's nailed the basic question. Is this something I want? High school isn't exactly the time you want to be different in a weird way. "I'm not sure. In some ways it's amazing and in some ways it scares me."

"Perhaps if you try to think of it as a gift, as something very positive, it won't be frightening." *Easy for you to say, Miss Practical.*

"You're probably right." I haven't even told her about the Universal Energy Field stuff. Dad would probably be more into that anyway. I get up and put my dishes in the sink. "I gotta go. Will's on his way over."

"How is Will doing? I haven't seen him around much lately."

"He's all right, I guess. He's kind of being a jerk, really."

"He must be dealing with a lot of things at home. Maybe cut him some slack."

I mumble something under my breath and go outside to wait for him. He's obviously dealing with a lot of crap at home, but does that mean that I have to put up with his crap? Driving in together in the morning and soccer practice are really the only times I see him anymore. He's so focused on being cool and hanging out with his new friends that he doesn't have much time or interest in me anymore. And I definitely can't talk to him about what's happening in the lab because he thinks it's all nuts and that I'm trying to weasel my way into the internship. Which is really funny because Will is so totally *not* focused on school or anything other than hanging out. I don't know if he's even applied for the internship. He may have moved on from our friendship, but he's still competing with me.

THE BELL RINGS for the end of first period. Renee leans back, lays her head on my desk, and looks up at me and smiles. Which starts that familiar slow burn inside my chest. At least one thing is going right for me. I lean forward and kiss her on the forehead.

We're still getting our books and backpacks together when Cole and Will come over from the back of the room.

"Has this guy been treating you right?" Cole asks Renee, putting his hand on my shoulder. "Because, if he hasn't, I am prepared to step in for him at any time."

I know he's just being Cole, and even if he's really half in love with Renee, he wouldn't ever actually do anything and I shouldn't be jealous, but this really bugs me. The warm feeling I had a minute ago quickly turns into a cold knot in the pit of my stomach. I'm not really the possessive type, but this feeling keeps coming up. It's not jealousy exactly, more like . . . fear.

She laughs and says, "Thanks, Cole, but I'm pretty happy with Eric." She looks at me and smiles. This eases the knot a little, but not entirely.

Will pushes past Cole to get to the door. "Hey, dude, move over. I've got to get to US History on the other side of school. I'll see you guys later."

"It was nice talking with you, too, Mr. Asplunth," Cole says to Will's retreating back.

"Is everything OK?" Renee asks, seeing Cole and me exchange looks.

"Yeah, everything's cool. Will's just being a jerk, that's all. Nothing new, though," I say as I hoist my backpack onto my shoulder.

"Are you sure?" she says, her voice trailing off, looking first at me and then at Cole, who just shrugs.

"Not a big deal, really. Don't worry about it," I say cheerfully, trying to avoid further discussion. "Here, I'll walk you to your next class." I gently propel her forward down the aisle toward the door. "I'll catch you at lunch, Cole."

"Au revoir, mes amis," he says.

Renee turns and says, "A bientôt!"

"What did you say?" I ask as we join the crush of students in the hallway.

"He said 'goodbye, my friends' and I said 'see you later.' It's nice to be able to speak French with someone besides my family."

"I guess," I say, but I can't shake that feeling of anxiety. What's that all about? Will's crappy attitude isn't helping my mood much either.

16

I JERK AWAKE when something smacks the back of my head.

Paul pulls out my ear buds and yells, "Dude, wake up! We're gonna be there in like ten minutes."

I groggily open my eyes and shake my head. Paul's walking up and down the aisle of the bus waking up the rest of the team. I'd grabbed a window seat on the bus and shoved my soccer bag against the window as a pillow and was asleep as soon as we pulled out of the parking lot at 7:00 a.m. Everyone else is crashed out too. I pull out my phone and check the time. It's a little after ten. Our game's at noon against Fort Ben.

I lean my head back against the seat and try to focus and visualize making great saves. Today's game is big both for the team and for me. It's my chance to really show what I can do, and my pre-game nerves are pretty bad. I know they won't really go away until my first touch of the ball during the game when I can stop thinking about being nervous and just play. Being nervous in the goal is about the worst thing you can be. I have to be totally relaxed and totally focused.

"Hey, big guy." Will leans over the seat in front of me. "It's our defensive unit today. *Shut out.*" He holds out his hand to fist bump me.

"Shut out," I say decisively and bump my fist into his.

"So, Fort Ben has a couple of strong strikers to watch out for, but no real stand out. They don't hesitate to take shots, so you'll need to be ready."

"I'm ready." I know that I can do this. Make the big saves. I've done it before. About a thousand times. "Hey, with you out there at center back, there won't be anything for me to save. We've got this."

"You got that right." Will turns back around in his seat.

I pull out a couple of granola bars from my bag and my water bottle. I won't get to eat again until after the game, hours from now.

We pull into the parking lot, gather our gear, and walk over to the field. After the usual stretching and warm-up, Coach Swenson has Brett and me warm each other up in the goal. He hasn't actually told us who's starting today, so it's possible that it could be Brett, but he's been pretty consistent with alternating us, so it should be my turn to play. I feel good—strong and loose—it feels good to get the first dives in and start hitting the ground. When the team lines up to take practice shots, I forget about being nervous; I'm too busy diving and punching and making saves.

The stands are filling up with fans. A lot of people came from Monroe because it's such an important game. Coach calls us over for the team talk and the lineup. I'm starting. *Yes.* But then my stomach starts clenching again with nerves, and I work on slow breathing. Paul comes over as we're lining up to jog across the field to the stands.

"You're gonna own the box today. You're the Beast," he says and punches me on the shoulder.

"Totally, dude."

We jog across the field and wave to the fans as they call out our names. Everyone is screaming and waving towels. The players all have our game faces on and are trying to stay focused and calm. My parents and Drew are here, Renee and Bonnie and Cole, too. Will's parents are both here, but not sitting together. Our side of the stands is covered in purple and white, Monroe's colors.

It's game time. I jog to my end of the field, fastening my gloves. My routine in the goal is always the same. I touch the sides of the goal and the crossbar and then stand in the center and do a few jumps to get loose. *Bring it.*

The play stays in midfield for a while, both teams fighting for possession. We're pretty evenly matched. I stay alert and watch the play, calling out marks to my team. Goalkeepers often end up making good coaches because we see all of the action and patterns of play, not just one portion of the field. It's a little like being the quarterback, except instead of calling plays, we direct the defense.

One of Fort Ben's strikers is cherry picking in the midfield, waiting for the pass so he can turn it toward the goal. Twice I've had to yell at my defenders to cover him. I'm about halfway into the penalty area so I can intercept a through ball, but still get back if I need to cover the goal. We've been battling for the ball on the right side of the field, and our players aren't having any luck gaining control.

"Switch!" I yell to my players to get them to swing the ball to the left side, where our midfielder is wide open.

Our center mid sends the ball across, but the Fort Ben striker makes a spectacular move and leaps into the air to win the ball. He quickly settles it and takes off, sprinting toward me and the goal. The distance between us narrows. My heart starts pounding, sending adrenaline coursing through me. If I run to meet him and he gets around me, it's a goal. Will has caught up with him and is pushing him wide left. I hold my line and cover the goal, anticipating the shot. He muscles past Will and is barreling full speed toward me. *The shot! Now! Dive!* It flashes into my head. *Make the save!*

He rips off a rocket to the far post. I'm propelled by a sudden surge of power, diving right, full out. I catch the ball in my gut and wrap my arms around it. A one-pound missile. Then, *wham*, the striker plows into me and nails me with a kick right in my ribs before he flips over and lands on his back on the hard-packed ground in the goalmouth.

I'm gasping for breath—it's like all the air has been sucked out of my lungs. There's a stabbing pain on my left side, but I've still got the ball. I made the save.

I lie there for a minute to catch my breath and gather myself. I had that feeling again. *Knowing* where the ball is going before the shot is taken. But there was something more this time. In the moment when I knew where the shot was going and what I had to do, I got a jolt of adrenaline or energy, or *something* that catapulted me off my feet. Goalkeeping starts with using your head to read the play, then moving your feet, and finishes with your hands. Whatever was going on in my head had let loose some powerful stuff this time.

"Are you OK?" Will is standing over me when I open my eyes.

"Yeah, I think so. Just a cracked rib, no problem," I say sarcastically. I reach out my hand and wince when he pulls me up.

"Shake it off." He claps me on the back. "Awesome save. That'll make him think twice before coming in close for a shot again." Will is looking right at the Fort Ben player and says this loud enough for him to hear. Just a little trash talk. The striker gets up off the ground and walks slowly up the field. He looks back at me warily. That's what I want to see. Fear.

I walk to the edge of the penalty box, bounce the ball three times, and take the punt. I know it's good when my foot connects with the ball. It sails seventy yards across the center line into the opposite end of the field. All my pre-game nerves are gone, washed away in the surge of adrenaline and the rush of making the save. Saving the first real shot on goal is critical. It energizes the team and keeps the momentum on your side. Not to mention making me totally stoked. I still feel the power coursing through me. I barely notice my ribs, but I'm sure I'll be sore after the game when all the other bruises and contusions start to appear.

We're putting the pressure on Fort Ben, keeping the play in their defensive third. It's a physical match with a lot of pushing and shoving that the ref isn't calling. Like they didn't call the foul on the striker when he plowed into me. Paul takes a shot, which is deflected wide by their keeper, giving us a corner kick. Dameon, our freshman holding midfielder, takes the corner and sends it in a perfect arc toward the goal. All the players leap into the air trying to get a head on it, but Paul gets there first and heads it into the goal. The ball zooms past the keeper and into the back of the net.

GOOOOAAAAL!!

Our team goes wild, mobbing Paul. The Monroe fans are screaming. The stands are a blur of purple and white towels waving furiously.

We keep the score at one to nothing until halftime. I'm pretty tired from making saves, but nothing I can't handle. I feel totally on my game today. I don't need to visualize now, it's real. Fort Ben is good, but so is Monroe, and so am I.

Coach Swenson calls the team over to a shady area at the end of the field for our halftime talk. I get one more cup of water from the big cooler on the sidelines and sit on the edge of the group in the back. Brett is up front, near Coach. I'm sure it sucks for him to watch me rocking the goal, but there's not much I can do about that.

"It's a well fought game; the teams are pretty evenly matched, but we have the upper hand and the momentum, so let's keep it that way," Coach Swenson is saying. "Offense needs to keep the pressure on and take shots. No hesitation. Don't hang onto the ball. One touch, pass or shoot. And keep switching the ball—diagonal balls are going to slice them open." Paul and Hernando, the other striker, nod. "Defense, keep doing what you're doing. Asplunth, you're doing a good job shutting down their striker, and Horton, you're keeping us on top. Don't let them get one past you."

The second half starts with Monroe taking the ball downfield and getting off a shot, but the Fort Ben keeper makes the save and punts it all the way to my penalty box. Will and Tyler, my other center back, collect the ball. Both teams keep the pressure on and play all out, but can't finish with a goal. We're still up one-nothing with five minutes left. The play's been aggressive on both sides and the refs have pretty much let it go. Now Fort Ben is getting desperate, and the play is brutal. Tyler's been battling with the Fort Ben striker in the backfield, and, between him and Will, they've been able to mostly shut him down. The striker is obviously frustrated and angry, which makes him dangerous.

In the last play of the game, their striker gets the ball and starts dribbling down the field. I try to judge if he's going to pass it off or try to score himself. I'm crouched and ready in the goal, coiled for action. Tyler runs on to him, trying to push him wide or get the ball. They're getting close to the penalty box when the striker comes down hard on Tyler's instep with his cleats and gives him a vicious elbow to the ribs.

Tyler drops like a rock, head over heels, and he takes the striker down with him. The ref blows the whistle and calls the foul, but it's on Tyler! *No way!* Will and the other Monroe players are yelling at the ref that the foul was on the striker, but the ref's already positioning the ball for a free kick. At least it's not a penalty kick—point blank at the goal. Two more steps and they would have been in the box.

"Wall! Four!" I yell, directing four guys on the wall to block their free kick. Will and Tyler and the two midfielders form the wall between me and the ball. I judge the angle of the striker. "Right, right! OK. Stop!" I'm not getting any feeling about where the ball is going, but I still feel the energy coursing through me. *Deep breath. Focus. Move to the center of the goal, get the angle right. Think—where's it going?* The striker's been playing it to the lower right corner all night, so I'm anticipating that shot. The ref blows the whistle.

The striker lines up to take the shot, runs onto the ball, and past it! A second player runs onto the ball to take the kick, and, just before he connects, it flashes in my head—*upper ninety, left corner!* I'd been thinking lower right corner, so I'm slightly out of position and off balance. Can I make it? *Don't think! Move!* He's left-footed, and he shoots, sending the ball with pace toward the center of the goal. Then it starts curving, bending to my left. I'm off the ground, flying, reaching—the tips of my fingers connect with the ball and I crash to the ground. It goes wide of the goal, but not far enough. I'm on my hands and knees scrambling to get to the ball—*where are my defenders?*—but the striker is on to it before I can collect it and he sends it past me into the goal, lower right corner. *Damn.*

The game ends in a tie. We're 14–0–1 for the season, not 15–0–0. No perfect season. None of the great saves I made matter when the one I miss means we didn't win the game. Of course, it wasn't my fault that the call went the wrong way and there was a free kick. And everyone knows that it's a team effort, but I'm the one who got scored on. Will and Tyler should have been there to clear the ball, but in the end I overthought it. And let them score.

We walk back to the bus deflated. The Fort Ben team is pumped, happy about avoiding a loss, but we were ahead almost the whole game and I let it slip away. I still have to act confident and cocky, so I don't look weak, but I feel like shit.

"Hey, dude, don't sweat it," Paul says, walking beside me. "It was a brutal game, and you saved like twenty shots. You can't save them all. Will and Tyler needed to shut that guy down. And that had to be a hometown ref."

"Whatever," I say. I'm pissed at myself, and I don't feel like being let off the hook. Somehow I need to figure out how to get out of my own way and not overthink the play. Let it just come to me. I'm not sure how to do it.

"Anyway, save it for the tournament. We could face them again if we make it to the finals, and we *will* shut them down."

The coaches pass out box lunches and drinks when everyone is back on the bus. Sub sandwich, chips, and an apple. It's always the same thing, but I'm starving, so I wolf it down and take four ibuprofen from the bottle in my bag. My ribs and various other places on my body are starting to hurt.

Oblivion is what I need. I shove my soccer bag against the window as a pillow and go right to sleep as the bus pulls out of the parking lot.

I dream that I'm in the goal saving shots. Will and some other faceless players are taking shots on goal. They're coming at me fast and furious, but I'm deflecting them easily. It's dark outside, and there are millions of stars in the sky overhead. The field is illuminated from a glowing fog that floats around it, on the edge of my vision. Now the shots are even faster, and they've become like comets, blazing down on me in fiery balls from the sky. I catch them and they explode in my hands, but my gloves protect me from the flames. Then the comets are raining down all around me in a hailstorm of bright, burning lights that cover the field. The dream morphs, and I'm walking with Renee through the woods at the lagoons. It's still night time and we're holding hands. I feel a strength and comfort from her touch. Up ahead we see an orange glow through the trees. It gets brighter as we approach. We step past the edge of the trees into the clearing, and before us is the stargazing rock rising up into the sky, glowing red and orange and gold in the night, hot and molten. It throbs with energy that bathes us in waves of power and light.

My phone buzzes in the bag under my head, waking me up. It's Renee texting me that she'll meet me at the concert tonight. I text back "OK" that I will see her there. She's going with friends from her AP Studio Art class to the PantheRock concert on the practice field behind the football stadium. All the garage bands from school try out to get a chance to play in the concert. Some of them are totally awesome and some of them suck. It's a big deal to the bands that get in, and we get to listen to some pretty tight music. I check the time on my phone. I've been asleep for almost two hours. My fingers tentatively probe my ribs. Definitely sore, but I don't think they're broken. I'll be purple and green by morning, though.

I could go to the concert with Paul and some of the other guys, but I might just go by myself so I have a car to take Renee home. Strange that she texted me right when I was dreaming about her. I want to tell her about the dream, but in person, not in a text. Maybe I'll tell her tonight about the other dreams, too. I haven't told anyone about them. Talking about them would have been like acknowledging them somehow. Giving them importance. At least in this one I didn't wake up screaming, and no one seemed in any danger. Those other dreams had started to freak me out a little . . . really more than just a little. What with the remote viewing and the astral projection, who knows what I was actually seeing in those dreams or if it was in any way real. This one was more cool than anything else. I'd felt like the energy from the comets and the stargazing rock was somehow part of me and that it was good energy. It gave me a feeling of power, and I'd had this wonderful, positive sense of everything being right. So why now, awake and sitting on the bus, do I still feel uneasy?

17

I END UP going to PantheRock with Paul, Tyler, and Will. Tyler has a Jeep Cherokee with a wicked sound system, and I can hear the bass coming in through the open windows of my bedroom when they pull up to the house.

My phone dings with a text from Paul. WE R HERE. WILL BROGHT A FLASK. *Great.* Now he's gonna be drinking on school grounds. I don't feel like dealing with this. Except for soccer, he's been totally blowing me off, so why should I be his babysitter?

GREAT . . . B RIGHT DN. I was actually surprised that Will wanted to go with us at all. It's probably because his "cool" friends started without him and he needed a ride.

When I climb into the back seat next to Will, he's leaning laconically against the opposite door with a cocky grin on his face. Paul turns around from the front seat and says angrily, "Normally I wouldn't give a crap what you do, but sectionals start next week, and we need you if we're gonna have a chance to win state. If you get kicked off the team for drinking, you're not just screwing yourself."

"Chill out, dude. It's just a little vodka. No one is gonna find out and no one is gonna get hurt."

"You don't know that," I say in a flat, determined voice. "You're way overdoing the whole 'party guy' thing. I mean a beer here and there is one thing, but a flask? What the hell is that about?" I hesitate and take a breath before I say, less harshly, "Acting like this isn't going to change anything about your dad, you know."

Will takes a sharp intake of breath and says in a low, mocking voice, "What the hell do you know about it? Did you use some of your 'magic powers' to see what's going on at my house or with my dad? How's that going for you, anyway? Didn't seem to help much with that last goal."

He couldn't have hurt me more if he had actually hit me. I recoil as if he did strike me. My best friend gives me a cold stare. I know he's dealing with the mess his dad left, but I'm done. I don't need to be his punching bag. I turn away from him and look out the window.

Paul jumps to my defense. "That was so low. We're supposed to be a team, remember? Have each other's backs. Eric's trying to help you, don't you get it?" He's practically in the backseat now, yelling at Will, but it doesn't do any good. Will pulls out the flask and takes a drink from it in defiance. Paul smacks the back of his chair and then turns back to the front. Tyler turns up the stereo as he pulls away from the curb. No one talks the rest of the way to school.

We have to wait in line for a few minutes to get to the admissions table. The show started at four, but the best bands don't play until 9:00 p.m., so people are really just starting to show up now. We pay our five bucks, and the mom sitting at the table hands us the band schedule. As soon as we're in, Will goes off on his own looking for his new friends, just like I thought he would.

"*Adios, amigos!*" He calls to us over his shoulder, "Don't wait up for me!" Even though he's being a jerk and I don't really want to hang out with him, it still hurts that he's moved on from our friendship. He's someone I thought I would always be able to count on. I guess there's no question of me watching his back now since he won't be around, and frankly, I don't much feel like it.

"That dude is messed up," says Paul. "We've got to keep an eye on him so he doesn't do something stupid."

"Good luck with that," I say and shove my hands in my pockets. "He doesn't want our help." We've moved to the back of the crowd to watch the band that's currently playing. The stage is set up at one end of the practice field, and booths from different school groups ring the fenced-in perimeter selling food, drinks, T-shirts, and stuff to raise money. The lights are on, but parts of the field are in shadows from the oncoming night. I scan the crowd hoping to get a glimpse of Renee, but there are too many people milling around. And she hasn't replied to the text I sent when we got here.

"Hey, check it out, Winston is setting up," Tyler says.

"Awesome, they rock." We know some of the guys in Winston, and they're pretty good. The lead singer was telling me at lunch on Friday that they are totally stoked about playing tonight because they've scored a good time slot and they're debuting a new original song.

They've been playing for about ten minutes when we notice that the percussionist is doing something with his hair.

"What's Steven doing to his hair?" Tyler asks.

"I think he's got a pair of scissors and he's cutting it!" Paul says, "Yeah, he totally is—check out the song lyrics—it's 'Cut Your Hair' by Pavement!"

"Holy crap, that is so awesome!" Steven's hair is longish and thick, and he's ratted it up on his head so it's big and bushy. "He's jabbing his hair with the scissors and cutting out chunks of it."

Then there's some kind of commotion on stage, and the music stops. Mrs. Stoat, the faculty advisor for the event, has appeared and is yelling at the band and gesturing at Steven and the floor of the stage.

"What's going on?" asks Tyler. "She looks pissed."

Now Mrs. Stoat has thrust a broom at Steven and he's sweeping up the chunks of hair that fell from his head. The band has started pulling their equipment from the stage.

"Oh, man, she made them stop playing. That sucks!" exclaims Paul.

My phone buzzes in my pocket. I fish it out hoping it's a text from Renee.

IM DOWN IN FRONT OF STAGE LEFT SIDE.

B RIGHT THERE. I text back.

"I'm going to meet up with Renee down by the stage. I'll catch up with you guys later."

"We'll come with you. I want to find out what happened with Winston and Mrs. Stoat." Paul is already pushing his way through the crowd.

Tyler and I follow Paul through the path he's making as he weaves his way toward the stage. I can see over the heads of most of the crowd, and now that I know where to look, I see Renee standing with a group of people just in front of the stage. Her glossy dark hair catches the light as she throws her head back and laughs at something one of them is saying.

"Hey, babe," I say quietly when I get up beside her and touch her lightly on the shoulder. She turns to me and smiles, which makes my heart jump, and then puts her hand on my hip and gets up on her toes to kiss me on the cheek, which makes my heart pound.

"We've been dancing," she says, and I see that little wisps of her hair are clinging wetly to her forehead and her face is slightly damp. She looks beautiful.

"Hmmm," I say and lean down to give her a kiss on the mouth. She kisses me back and then pulls away when one of her friends says, "Hey, too much PDA here!"

Renee looks up at me with her eyes crinkling at the corners and says, "Would you like to meet my friends?"

"OK," I say and turn to them, but I really want to talk to Renee alone about my dreams.

"This is Miles and Anna and Emily. We're in AP Studio Art together." I recognize them from the party the night we went to the stargazing rock. It's the guy with the nasty vibe and the hipster look, and the girl with the long red hair and army boots.

"Hey," I say and nod to them. "Do you mind if I steal Renee away for a minute?" To Renee I say more quietly, "Can I talk to you alone. I want to tell you something."

I take her wrist and gently pull her over to the side of the stage. "That was totally abrupt," she says. "I wanted you to meet my friends and *talk* to them."

"I'm sorry, we can go back in a minute, but I want to tell you about this wild dream I had on the ride home from the game. You were in it."

"Really, what were we doing?" she says, poking me in the gut and implying something entirely different than what I meant.

"Not *that* kind of dream. We were walking in the woods at the lagoons, holding hands, and the stargazing rock was glowing, almost burning. I could feel a sort of emotional strength from you and an incredible power or energy from the rock. The weird thing is that it felt so real. Even when I'm remembering it now, it feels like it actually happened and wasn't just a dream."

"Do you think it was energy from The Field? You felt something there before. That's pretty wild."

"I'm not really sure, but, yeah, it could be something like The Field. There's more—I've been having these other dreams. Really freakin' crazy dreams with explosions and fire. I haven't wanted to think too much about them because they pretty much scare the crap out of me, so I haven't told anyone."

"Do you think they mean something?"

"That's the thing, I have no idea."

We're off to one side of the stage, in a little alcove to stay out of the way of the bands setting up and tearing down equipment for their shows. Renee has her back to the wall, and I'm standing between her and the activity, so I don't see Paul and Tyler come up behind me with Steven from Winston.

"Eric, you gotta hear this," Paul interrupts us. "Steven says Mrs. Stoat told him that cutting his hair on stage was a health hazard and that he should be ashamed of himself! She made them quit playing before they got to play their new song."

"That sucks. What does she mean—a health hazard? Unbelievable," I say.

"Yeah, right?" Steven says. "She's a total buzz-kill. Of all the things we could be doing, and she freaks about me cutting my hair." He runs a hand through his hair and little pieces of it flutter down around his face. I can see where the chunks are missing.

"No shit. It's not like you were doing shots or lighting up or anything. And the lyrics weren't inappropriate. Why are some teachers so cool and the rest don't get it?" Paul is really pissed.

"Who knows. She's wound just a little too tight. I mean it's great that she's helping with PantheRock and all, but she needs to lighten up," says Steven. The next band setting up is one of the headliners. They've got three vocalists and a horn section and they're a fantastic cover band.

"Strategy's up next," I say. "Let's go down in front so we can see better." I turn to Renee. "We can go stand with your friends, and you can dance some more," I say with a smile.

She leads me by the hand back to the pseudo mosh pit. I feel better just having told her about the dreams. It's not like I thought we'd come to some insightful conclusion, but it's nice to have someone else know and even understand. She asked me what they mean, but I really don't know. And frankly, given what they are, I'm not sure I ever want to find out.

The first song Strategy plays is a great dance tune. The crowd is whooping and cheering as we get to the front of the stage where Anna, Emily, and Miles are dancing and watching the band. Anna squeals, "Hey girl!" and moves to the side to make room for us. All around us people are bumping and grinding to the beat. Renee stays next to me for a while, and then moves over to dance with Emily, who whispers something in her ear, making Renee laugh.

That leaves Anna beside me, and she starts whipping her hair around and bumping me with her hip. I'm not sure how to take this—is she just including me in the group or is she coming on to me? You'd think that I'd be better at reading girls' intentions, given that I'm supposed to be perceptive about people, but I'm at a total loss. Now Miles is dancing with Renee and Emily, and it's clear what his intentions are. He's totally focused on Renee. I can see it in his body language and how he's raking her up and down with his eyes. But it's more than that. Most guys are always checking girls out, but something about Miles bugs me. A lot.

I maneuver around Anna and Emily to get next to Renee. Miles is on Renee's far side, so at least I can keep an eye on him better from this vantage point. All my scrapes and bruises from the game are starting to throb as the ibuprofen wears off, and the dancing is jarring my ribs. I'm used to working through pain, but I wouldn't mind leaving now with Renee. Maybe I can get Tyler to give us a ride home.

There's a lull in the music as Strategy clears off stage and the next band sets up, so I ask Renee, "Do you want to head out now? I'm pretty sore from the game today. Maybe we could go hang out someplace where I can sit down for a while."

"There's still two more bands left to play, and I want to dance!" she says. "Maybe you could go hang out by the booths for a while. I think people are sitting on the grass back there."

I can tell she's having a great time, and I'm about to say I can meet up with her later, when Miles drapes his arm across Renee's shoulder, pulling her into him and says, "Yeah, my girl's gonna stay here and dance the last sets with me, aren't you?" He's breathing hard from dancing, and it's almost like he's panting in anticipation. Renee looks startled at first and then laughs to cover it. The hairs on the back of my neck rise up, and I feel like his gaze is a challenge. I've never been one to shy away from a challenge.

I take a step closer to him so he has to tilt his head back to look up at me. "She's not your girl—take your hands off her." I knock his arm off her shoulder. He gives me a look of mock chagrin and says to Renee. "Hey, I'm sorry, Renee, I wasn't coming on to you or anything. It's just friends. I know you want to dance, that's all."

"Of course, Miles, it's fine. I do want to dance," she says and pats him on the chest. "Eric, what's your problem?" she demands, pulling me away from the group. When we get a few feet away, she turns on me angrily. "Miles is my friend, what are you doing?"

"He's bad news. I could tell the first time I saw him. And I know you weren't totally cool with what he did back there. I saw your face. I don't want you to hang out with him anymore." As soon as I say this, I realize it's a mistake. Renee's not the kind of person who will tolerate being ordered around, and it's not like I really want to tell her what to do. I rub my forehead with my hand as if it will clear my brain. I'm really tired from the game, from everything.

"Are you telling me who I can be friends with? You don't own me." She puts her hands on her hips defiantly. "And you're wrong about Miles. You don't even know him. He's a really nice guy, just a little awkward, that's all."

I reach to grab her hands, but she pulls them away. I shove my hands in my pockets, exasperated. "I'm sorry, that came out wrong. You can be friends with whoever you want. It's just that I've had a bad feeling about him since that first party we went to. I can't explain it, but it's like somehow I know he's a jerk. More than a jerk. I just don't want him to cause trouble for you."

"What kind of trouble could he possibly cause? All the remote viewing has made you think you know more than you really do. That was totally out of line back there. You embarrassed me in front of my friends, and you have no right to tell me what to do." I can't believe how pissed off she is about this. I may have gotten angry at Miles, but I didn't think it was that bad. Then she says, "I'm going to go back to dance with my friends the rest of the night." She emphasizes *my friends*. "Maybe you should go ahead and go home." Now I really can't believe what she's saying. I feel like a giant weight's been placed on my shoulders.

"You want me to leave?" I ask, not wanting to accept that this is happening.

"I'm just going to stay with the people I came with, and you can hang out with your soccer friends. I'll talk to you tomorrow." Then she turns and walks back to Anna, Emily, and Miles, leaving me standing there, alone in the middle of the sea of students. I feel a dull ache in my heart. Miles is looking at me, and I could swear he's giving me a sneer of triumph.

I look away from him and turn my gaze skyward. I think about following Renee, but I don't want to make a scene in front of everyone, and she did say she would talk to me tomorrow. Maybe she won't be as upset by then. The next band is playing now, and all around me people are moving to the beat, jostling me as I stand in what feels like an island of stillness, numb. Then the pain starts radiating out in waves in my chest, and I can't catch my breath because it feels like a hand is squeezing all the air out of my lungs. Is this what heartache feels like? I turn and push through the crowd toward the exit. I don't have a clear idea of what I'm going to do. I just want to get out of there. Meeting up with Tyler and Paul isn't an option since I'm in no mood to talk to anyone, and they're bound to ask me what's wrong. It's only a couple miles to my house, so I'm thinking I'll just walk home.

I have to zigzag past groups of people to get to the back. The crowd thins out as I get closer to the booths where people are milling around and paying less attention to the band. I stop for a minute to get my bearings on where the exit is, and over to my left I see Will out of the corner of my eye. What catches my attention is that his hair has fallen over his eyes and he does the familiar gesture of pushing it back with his hand. He's with the same crowd he's been hanging out with lately and is obviously having a good time. Great. Another thing that sucks about my life right now. I look the other direction and see the exit gate to my right. When I pass the woman at the ticket table she says, "There's no re-entry to the concert once you leave."

"Thanks. I'm not coming back."

I walk quickly across the parking lot. Once I leave the lights of the field and the parking lot behind me, I'm plunged into darkness. I'm grateful for the anonymity of the night. It's gotten windy, so I zip up my jacket, put my hands in my coat pockets, and hunch my shoulders against the chill. How did everything get so crappy? Will is being wild and acting like a jerk most of the time, I have to compete for the starting keeper spot and prove myself in every game, so every time I let in a goal I feel like I've blown it, and now my girlfriend is mad at me. I'm working so hard trying to figure out the collective consciousness stuff, and I can't seem to get it. Maybe Renee's right, and I don't really know anything. That seemed like a betrayal coming from her, especially after Will attacked me with the same thing. If she doesn't believe in it, why should I? Did I do better in the goal before I tried to focus on knowing where the shots were going to go? I'm probably overthinking it. I don't know. It doesn't seem to be working, that's for sure.

My footfalls make a rhythmic sound on the sidewalk as I trudge along and an occasional leaf crunches under my shoe. It's still a little too early for the leaves to change, but fall is definitely here. There's a crispness in the air and the sweet fermenting smell of decaying summer plants. I stop at a corner and wait to cross until a car passes. My ribs are really aching now. The ibuprofen wore off a long time ago.

Finally, I turn the corner onto my street. The walk hasn't done much to improve my mood. I feel pretty useless—the guarded excitement I had the other day about the astral viewing with Drew and connecting to The Field with Dr. Auberge has turned to apathy and disbelief. I just want to go to bed and forget everything. My house is shrouded in gloom because no one's turned on the outside lights, and the light at the end of the driveway is off. I gratefully reach the driveway, and just when I step under the street light, it abruptly lights up, shining into the darkness and illuminating me in a circle of light.

18

Mr. Ogle leads us to a door at the end of the science hallway that I never paid attention to before. He stops in front of it with his hand on the handle and says, "It's worth repeating that you must *stay away from the edge of the roof.* If one of you falls, that will be the end of classes getting to go up here, not to mention being very painful for you." He inserts a key into the lock, opens the door, and climbs the stairway going up to the roof. The students file in behind him.

Will, Cole, Renee, and I have formed an awkward group at the back of the line. Awkward because Will isn't really associating with us except for during class and on the soccer field, and because things are still tense between me and Renee. I tried to explain to her on Sunday why I was concerned about Miles, but she just thinks I'm jealous and don't trust her. We're not exactly fighting, but it's not the same between us. Cole isn't helping matters by simply being Cole and making snide remarks.

"Eric, don't you feel a draft in this hallway? It could be a bit of cold shoulder, if you know what I mean," he says, low enough that only I can hear him. I'm not sure if he means Will or Renee. Probably both.

"Shut up, Cole. It's bad enough without your sarcastic comments."

I climb the stairs behind Renee and pass through the doorway at the top and onto the roof of the school. The wind whips across the wide open expanse, catching the tails of my shirt and making them flutter. The roof is tarred and covered with pebbles, which crunch under my shoes as I follow the rest of the class over to the solar panels. There are three rows of panels with eight sections per panel.

"The student environmental club runs the paper, plastic, and aluminum can recycling program here at school and uses the proceeds to fund its activities." Mr. Ogle is standing to the side of the panels and is turned toward the class. He has to speak loudly to be heard over the humming of giant fans positioned at intervals across the roof. "Every year the students in the club set aside money to go toward different environmental programs they support. A portion of the funds is also earmarked for purchasing solar panels for the school, so when enough money has accumulated, we get new panels."

"What do the panels power?" a boy toward the front asks.

"With a building this large, three panels can't do too much, but the energy generated from these panels is able to heat the water used in the cafeteria. The energy gathered over the summer, when the cafeteria isn't used, is sold back to the utility, which gives the school energy credits to use during the school year."

I'm standing behind Renee, and I have to stop myself from putting my hands on her shoulders and pulling her against me. Her hair is blowing around her head, and strands of it fan across my face. I don't try to push them away. It's not that I think she wouldn't want me to touch her, it's just that this isn't really the place. But I've only seen her alone once since Sunday because of soccer practice and sectional games this week. Now that the tournament has started, I don't have much free time between soccer and homework to see her. We studied together at the library on Tuesday, but there wasn't much opportunity to be alone. She just gave me a quick kiss goodbye when I dropped her off. It feels awful that things aren't right between us, and I miss being with her. I don't know what I can do to make it better. Especially since I still don't like her hanging out with Miles and I can't say anything.

Will elbows me in the side to get my attention. "Nice shut out against Winchester last night. Now it's just regionals and semistate to get to the final. Think we can do it?"

"Thanks." Soccer's the only thing we talk about now. I played a decent game against Winchester, but there wasn't really much for me to do. And I was playing more by rote than by instinct. I've been questioning the whole collective consciousness stuff, and it's making me overthink everything in the goal. Fortunately, our defense did its job, shutting down Winchester's offense so I only had a few big saves to make. And I did save them. It wasn't much of a contest—we won four to nothing. "Bloomfield's our next match and they're tough, but yeah, I think we can do it. We've got the players . . . I think we definitely have a chance at state this year."

Mr. Ogle is still talking. "I'm sure you're aware that the high school doesn't have a lot of windows." Some of the kids up front nod in agreement. "What you may not know is that it's because the school was renovated and expanded back in the 1970s during the energy crisis. Not having windows was an attempt to lower energy costs. But it's like going to school in a box. No natural light."

"Totally!" someone shouts out.

"I think solar panels are a much better energy saving program, as they allow the school to create its own energy. The roof is the perfect place for solar panels because it's flat and tall and they can't be seen from the ground."

Yet another alternative to burning fossil fuel. Why wouldn't you embrace these other energy sources? It just requires the initial investment. I guess change is hard for people. I know there are tax credits for green energy, but maybe if there were stricter penalties for polluting that were actually enforced there would be more incentive to change. Mr. Ogle continues talking about solar energy for another few minutes and then we go back to the classroom, where he finishes the lecture.

Instead of sitting in the back where he and Will usually sit, Cole takes the seat across the aisle from Renee. When the bell rings and everyone starts gathering up their stuff, he leans over to her and says, "I reiterate my offer of an evening out if you ever want to dump this guy here." He jabs his thumb in my direction. "He can act pretty stupid sometimes."

Renee looks quizzically from Cole to me, probably wondering what I told Cole about our fight. I haven't actually told him anything. He's just perceptive enough to pick up on the tension between us. Maybe he's trying to be funny, or maybe he's trying to help in his screwed-up way, I don't care. I just know that I have to keep it light and not get pissed at him even though I want to strangle him at the moment.

"Thanks, Cole, I'll, ah, keep that in mind," Renee says in a way that's nice, but also totally blowing him off. I let out a breath of air that I didn't realize I was holding in.

"I'll see you later, Cole," I say pointedly. But what I really mean is—leave now.

"Don't forget—applications for the internship have to be turned in by Monday," Mr. Ogle calls out. "Interviews will be scheduled after fall break."

I take a step closer to Renee. "Maybe we could go to a movie or something tonight," I ask her. "Are you coming to the regional game tomorrow?"

"Do you know if you're starting?"

"Coach Swenson hasn't actually said that he's going with me in the tournament, but so far I've started two games in a row. I hope you can come."

"Yes, I'll be there. And I'd like to go to a movie tonight, too."

"Great!" I breathe a sigh of relief. I was half afraid she'd say no. Maybe everything doesn't totally suck.

19

I PUSH MY chair back from the table and take the electrodes off of my forehead. Tonight I'd been able to light up the second bulb on the panel for over five seconds—the longest time yet. Steven is at my side in an instant checking the data records on the computer.

"That was great, Eric. You're getting the hang of it for sure." It's just the two of us in the lab tonight. "Do you want to try again?"

"No, I'm done for the night. I've had soccer every night this week and I'm wiped out. I was only able to stop by tonight because Coach gave us the day off. We won our first semistate game last night. Our next game is Saturday. If we win, we're in the state final." I say this without much emotion because it's not like I think Steven is a fan or anything, but he surprises me.

"That's fantastic! You're the keeper, right? Dr. Auberge is pretty into soccer and he's been telling me that you might be tapping into collective consciousness when you play. Of course, the whole town knows about it too."

"They do?" I say, slightly alarmed.

"Not about the collective consciousness stuff," he says quickly. "About the team winning in the tournament. You guys are like local heroes."

"Oh, right. One of the benefits of living in a small town." I pick at a frayed piece of black electrical tape on the edge of the table. "So what do you really think about all this?" I gesture to all the equipment in the room.

"You mean the experiments?"

"That, and the whole collective consciousness, and The Field, all of it. Do you think it's really real?"

"Well, yeah, I do. That's why I'm here, but unfortunately, I haven't developed any heightened ability. Why, don't you think it's real?"

"When I'm here in the lab, I do, but back in my real life, it's hard to believe or to trust myself. Even here, I'm just lighting up light bulbs and making meters move and logging random thoughts into the computer. Nothing all that amazing. When I'm with other people, I'm just getting odd, unexplained feelings about things, and half the time no one takes it seriously. I even feel like I've lost it in the goal because I'm thinking about it so much. I'm still a good keeper, but the extra spark isn't there anymore."

"Believe me, I know it's hard to be different," he says, pointing to himself. "I'm sure it's especially hard when you think you know something that someone else doesn't want to hear." He scoots his chair around so that he's facing me. "I can tell you that The Field is very real. Even though it doesn't seem like much, you are connecting with it."

"Maybe, but I don't really know how I'm doing it."

"You might be working too hard at it. Instead of trying to force it, or understand it intellectually, you could try just opening yourself up to it. Accepting it. It's not just science, you know.

There's a very mystical aspect to all of it that we haven't even begun to understand."

This sounds strange coming from Steven, who looks more stork-like and geeky than ever tonight with his gangly arms sticking out at odd angles from his lab coat and his black horn-rimmed glasses. Not the person you'd expect to be talking about mystical things, but I find it oddly reassuring.

"Thanks, Steven. That means a lot." I gather up my backpack from the floor next to my chair. "I'll try to come in next week, but it'll be iffy."

"No problem. Knock 'em dead in the goal. Maybe I'll come to the game." Then, after a pause, he says, "May the force be with you," and *bows* to me. "I've always wanted to say that to someone and really mean it!" he says, almost giddy.

I'm smiling to myself as I walk away, trying to imagine Steven as Obi-wan Kenobi to my Luke Skywalker.

Nah.

20

A SHOT ZINGS toward me, and I parry it easily by lunging to my left and pushing the ball wide with my hand. It's Saturday afternoon—fifteen minutes into the semistate game—and the score's 0–0. Coach started me again and as much as I was glad, when I saw Brett's pained look of resignation I couldn't help but feel bad for him. He's a senior, and this may be his last shot at playing. Still, I would never trade places with him.

Will collects the ball and moves it downfield. He passes it to Raul, center midfielder. Raul likes to hang on to the ball and dribble it too long instead of passing. That's exactly what he does this time, and the midfielder from the other team muscles him out of the way and takes the ball. Then he sends a nice diagonal ball right on the money, leading his striker toward the goal. The striker takes a touch to settle the ball and gets off a low driving shot to the left corner. I'm ready, bouncing on the balls of my feet, anticipating the shot.

I dive left and feel my hand connect with the ball, and then a sharp, stabbing pain shoots up my arm as my hand slams into the goalpost, hyperextending my fingers.

I roll up onto my knees and hold my hand between my legs. *Shit.* The pain is making me disoriented. *I need to get up.* The ball went out of bounds and the ref's signaling for a corner kick. The play never stops. I start to get up and then my head clears a bit and I think, *No, stay down. Signal to the ref.* I kneel back down and raise my right hand, signaling that I'm injured. I hunch over in pain, waiting for the throbbing to subside. Sometimes it's hard to tell how badly you're injured until the initial stab of pain starts to fade. Even though I want to, it hurts so badly I can't get up and play yet.

The ref and my defenders run over to me. "Are you hurt? Are you able to play?" the ref asks. Will and Tyler look anxiously down at me. "Do you need the trainer?"

"No, just give me a minute," I say, and I hope it's true. The fingers of my left hand are still throbbing, but the pain is lessening. I've played with jammed fingers before. I can tough this out.

"OK," I say after another thirty seconds, my jaw tight with the effort of exerting my mind over the matter of my hand. "I'm good now." I stand up and shake out my arms. The ref signals for the corner kick and the players get into position in front of the goal.

Will comes closer before moving into position for the corner. "You sure you're OK?" he asks. I know what he's thinking. I can't be less than 100 percent in the goal.

"Yeah, I'm good. Just a jammed finger. I'll tape it up at half time." *There is no way I'm coming out now.*

The ref blows the whistle, and the other team positions the ball and takes the kick. Players from both teams are crowded in front of the goal, pushing and shoving and trying to get into position to get to the ball first. I've got my head back in the game now, and the adrenaline surging through me masks the pain in my hand.

The ball comes flying toward the mass of surging players, and they leap into the air, trying to get a head on the ball. A player from the other team, the tips of his hair bleached white, rises above the others and connects, heading it toward the goal. I see it coming and reach to catch it. I have both hands out to grab it and I'm in a good position. The ball isn't going too fast, but as it hits, the fingers on my left hand explode in pain. I can't hold onto the ball. Instead of catching it, the ball drops to the ground right at the feet of an opposing player. He starts to take a shot and even though pain is shooting from my hand up my arm, instinct kicks in and I fall onto the ball. I make the save but also get kicked in the side as he follows through with his cleats.

This can't be happening. I can't get injured in the tournament. I know I should come out, but I just can't. *At halftime I'll load up on ibuprofen and tape my fingers together.* I'll be fine.

I get up and walk to the edge of the box to take the punt. Players from both teams are moving back to the other end of the field. Except for Will and Tyler. They're still in our penalty area and they're both giving me hard, questioning looks. Which I ignore. I take the punt and move back into position. When I glance over toward the sideline, I see Brett warming up with another player.

The play stays pretty much at the other end of the field, keeping me out of danger and giving me time to pull it together. Raul makes an awesome lofted pass over the top to Dameon, who settles the ball and shoots, scoring for us. *Good. Up one.* I watch Brett on the sideline, now diving and making saves, but Coach Swenson hasn't subbed him in with the field players, so I'm not sure what to think. When I let my left hand hang by my side, it throbs with pain, so I hold both my hands in front of me like I'm ready to make a save. *I can do this.*

After our goal, the other team is hungry for one of their own. Teams at this level of the tournament are top notch and usually don't let themselves get down after being scored on. At the kickoff, they keep possession of the ball in midfield and pass it down the wing toward my end of the field.

The same striker who took the two shots earlier receives a perfect pass from a guy on the wing. He's wide open. *Who left him unmarked?* I feel an unwelcome sense of fear creep into my gut. He turns and fires, sending a whistling rocket to the same place as before, lower left corner.

I'm off my feet quick, diving to make the save, but part of me hesitates because I'm afraid of the pain. I barely get to the shot in time, stopping it with the fingertips of my left hand, but instead of pushing it wide, my injured fingers give way and the ball slips past me, into the goal.

I get up slowly from the hard-packed ground. My hand is throbbing, but I don't really notice it. The other team is celebrating the goal. *This is my fault.* I let my teammates down. I look up and see the subs running in from the sideline during the break in play. Brett is with them, waving me off.

I jog off the field, passing Brett on the way. We fist bump but don't say anything. There's nothing to say. For him, this is like a dream come true. For me it's a nightmare.

Coach Swenson sends me to the trainer when I reach the sideline. "Get that hand looked at," he commands. Not angrily, but not nicely, either. I walk to the end of the bench where the trainer is set up next to the cooler of water. I can't even get myself a drink because I can't bend the fingers of my left hand enough to hold the paper cup. I press the button on the faucet with my right hand, but when the liquid hits the cup, it slips from my fingers, spilling water onto the grass at my feet.

"Here, sit down." The trainer, Shelley, a sports medicine student from the university, says, "Let's get a look at your hand

and then I'll get you some water." She undoes the Velcro at the wrists of my gloves and pulls off the right one first. "How bad does it hurt?" she asks before pulling off the left glove.

"It hurts," is all I say. "Pull it off slowly." I take deep, slow breaths as she pulls off the glove. Partly because it hurts, but mostly because I'm trying not to lose it.

Shelley gives a final tug and pulls off the glove. My ring finger and middle finger are swollen and turning black and blue. "Can you move your fingers?" she asks. I tentatively curl my fingers toward my palm, but get only about a third of the way before I feel a stabbing pain. She manipulates them a bit herself and then covers my hand with a towel, puts a big bag of ice on top, and then wraps the whole thing in an ace bandage. "It's hard to tell for sure if they're jammed, sprained, or broken. You need an X-ray. Keep it iced and elevated." She gets me the cup of water and then leaves me alone. *Broken, broken, broken* reverberates in my head over and over.

I watch the rest of the game in a daze. Other players come to see how I'm doing, but I barely talk to them. Brett plays really well. In the second half, he makes a spectacular diving save on a shot that looked like it was going in. Will and Tyler yell encouragement at him. Which feels like a betrayal.

We end up winning 3–1. We made it to the championship game. I'm as happy as the rest of the team, but I'm also devastated. Brett had a shut-out and he's totally pumped coming off the field. He took his opportunity and made the most of it. Every keeper who's ever sat on the bench knows that he has to be ready to play in case the starter gets injured and can't play. *Can't play.* I don't even want to think about it. *They're just jammed. I'll be ready to play in the championship game.*

After the game, my parents and Marcie and Drew hurry across the field to see what happened. Renee follows behind.

"Are you OK? What happened?" my mom asks, unable to hide the worry in her voice.

"We saw you hit your hand on the post," my dad adds.

I lift my bag onto my shoulder with my good hand and hold up my left hand, which looks huge because of the ice bag. "I jammed my fingers pretty bad. The trainer says I need an X-ray." I try to keep my voice neutral, but they know what this could mean. They've been to enough soccer games and seen their share of injuries over the years.

Renee comes up and puts her hand on my right arm. "I'm sorry," she says quietly. I look down at her and see the concern reflected in her eyes. I try to give her a weak smile, but I think it comes off as more of a grimace.

"Here," my dad says, reaching for my bag and taking charge. "I'll get that." To my mom he says, "Jill, see if the coach will let us take Eric home instead of riding on the bus. I can drop you and Drew and Marcie at home and then take Eric to the ER for an X-ray."

Renee ends up riding home in the van with my family and going to the ER with me and my dad. I feel a little stupid sitting in the ER waiting room with all the really sick and injured people. It's not like I have a life-threatening injury or anything. But I actually do feel sick to my stomach.

In the examination room, after I've been taken for an X-ray and we've been there over two hours, the doctor clips the X-ray of my hand to the light box on the wall. "Well, I have good news and bad news, young man," he says. I'm still in my soccer uniform and have dirt smeared down the left side of my body. At least I was able to change out of my cleats into turf shoes. "The bad news is that your middle finger and ring finger both have hairline fractures." My stomach clenches.

"What's the good news?" my dad asks.

"The breaks aren't significant enough to stop you from playing—if you tape them together and you can deal with the pain." *All right. I can deal with pain.*

He puts a metal splint lined with blue foam cushioning onto the two fingers and tapes them together with the splint. I get a prescription for painkillers and a note for the coach that I'm cleared to play. The thing is, I can't wear the splint to play. As we leave the hospital, I'm thinking that I'll have to tape the two fingers of my glove together so I can play, and that I'll be able to do this, no problem.

But my dad has other ideas. "I know how important it is to you to play," he says as we pass through the automatic doors to the parking lot. Dusk has fallen while we were inside and the overhead lights are on. "But in the long run it's more important that your fingers heal properly. I don't want you to try to play before you're really ready." Renee is holding my right hand and she gives it a little squeeze, but I'm not sure if it's because she agrees with my dad or because she knows how I feel about playing. We get to the Audi, and my dad looks at me meaningfully over the roof as he unlocks the doors.

I open the back door and slide across the seat to sit next to Renee. "You heard what the doctor said," I tell him. "I can play if I tape my fingers. This might be my only chance to play in the championship game. Anyway, it doesn't matter because the final decision isn't even mine. It's Coach Swenson's." After how Brett played today, I don't know if I'll get a chance to play even if my fingers heal in time.

ON THE DRIVE home my dad calls my mom to tell her the diagnosis. "Your mom says she'll have dinner ready when we get home."

"Do you want to come over for dinner?" I ask Renee. "I can take you home later. I don't really feel like going out tonight, if that's OK with you." I reach across my body with my uninjured hand to grasp her hand. "Thanks for coming to the hospital with me, by the way. I'm sorry I'm not in a better mood."

"Yes, I'd like to come for dinner. We can just hang out; maybe watch a movie or something. I understand," she says brightly. I know she's trying to cheer me up, but I'm feeling pretty sorry for myself at the moment.

"Yeah, that sounds good." I lean my head back onto the seat. "What really sucks about this is that I actually made it to this point, the point that every kid who plays soccer hopes for. To be a starter and to get to the championship game. But it could be snatched right out from under me."

"Won't you be able to play? The doctor cleared you."

"Maybe—I don't know. Brett played really well tonight and it all depends on what Coach decides. It's totally out of my control."

Paul and Tyler and some of the other guys are texting me to find out how I'm doing. No text from Will, of course. I give them the details and tell them I'll see them on Monday. I don't want to talk to anyone. I just feel like lying low.

21

THERE'S A COLD drizzle falling as I walk out to the field for practice on Monday. I head straight to Shelley and give her the doctor's note. She has to clear me to play.

"He said I can play if I tape my fingers," I tell her. She doesn't need to know the part about "dealing with the pain."

She reads the note and then looks at me for a moment. She knows what's at stake. "OK, we'll tape you up and then you can tell Coach Swenson you're cleared." While she's putting tape around my gloved fingers, Paul and Tyler come over to see how I'm doing. They're wearing warm-up jackets and hats and gloves against the rain. If it weren't the week before the championship game, practice would probably have been cancelled because the weather is so crappy.

"How're they feeling?" Paul asks.

"Not bad. Maybe a little sore," I admit. "Nothing I can't handle." I had my dad throw the ball to me a little yesterday to see how it felt and the pain was manageable. I'm pretty sure I can take the real shots, too.

Will approaches us at that moment and overhears me. "That's what you thought on Saturday when you didn't come out. It cost us a goal." He says flatly. "It could've cost us the game." Even though what he's saying is basically true, it doesn't make it any less harsh.

"Maybe," I say, and stand up to face him. "But there wouldn't have been a shot if you'd marked your man." Will is tall, but I'm still a couple of inches taller and at least twenty pounds heavier. We stand there for a minute just staring at each other, and for once Paul doesn't say anything. Shelley's working on another player, so she's not paying any attention to us.

Eventually Will says, "It may not matter anyway, with the game only six days away." Then he turns to join the other players on the field. *WTF? Is he hoping I won't heal in time to play?*

"What the hell is with him?" says Paul.

"No kidding," adds Tyler. "He's being a total jackass."

"I have no idea," I say. The only thing I can guess is that maybe our once friendly rivalry has turned into something much more for Will. I can't let his issues affect me. "Not my problem. I've gotta talk to Coach."

I leave them and walk down the sideline to where he's talking with the assistant coaches and watching the warm-ups. They're talking about strategy for Fort Ben. That's who we'll be playing in the final. When I reach them, Coach Swenson turns to me.

"Eric, how's your hand? What'd the doctor say?"

"I have a hair-line fracture, but he and Shelley cleared me to play. I just have to tape my fingers." I hold up my hand to show him.

"Well, I'm glad it's not too serious. As long as it doesn't affect how you play. We'll see how you do in practice this week, and then decide who's starting on Saturday."

"I'm ready to play," I tell him.

"I'm glad to hear it," he says and then turns back to the other coaches, ending the discussion. *OK. I have to earn the starting spot again.*

I walk toward the goal where one of the field players is working with Brett. With each step, I take a deep breath and let it out slowly. I'm going to need all the sports psychology visualization techniques I know to do this. What I really need, though, is to somehow find that missing spark of *knowing*. I need to figure out how to consciously connect to The Field.

22

ON THE WAY home from dropping Renee off, I take a detour to the lagoons. I'm so wiped out that I want to chill a little before I go home. In practice all week, I played full out, giving everything I've got. Each day my fingers felt a little better, and now they aren't bothering me much at all, but the spark hasn't been there for me. I'm a great keeper even without any "extra" perceptions, so I controlled the goal and made the saves. I don't think anyone would have said I wasn't totally on my game, but I knew. The flash of insight that I've taken for granted wasn't there. The final is tomorrow, and Coach Swenson still hasn't told me and Brett who's starting. I have no idea which way it will go.

I park in the lot and when I get out of the car not one but two overhead lights go out. *Fine,* I think, sending a message up to the night sky, *but show me how I can control it.*

Walking along the path to the clearing and the lake reminds me of my dream and walking here with Renee. That's part of the reason I came. There's something special about the stargazing rock. It's not something I can define, exactly, but I just feel better when I'm here. More clearheaded and happier. It looms up in front of me, a dark silhouette against the grey sky. The newly risen crescent moon provides enough light for me to see the footholds of the stairway worn into the rock. When I get to the top, I stand for a moment and look out over the lake. The surface of the water is smooth and unrippled, and the moonlight illuminates a path across its surface that seems to end at the base of the rock. There's a quiet stillness surrounding the lake. Only the sounds of frogs and crickets making a rhythmic buzz can be heard from the far shore. I stretch my arms high over my head and arch my back. It feels like all the tension I'm holding in my body flows out through my fingertips and up into the sky.

I lie down on the flat surface of the rock and close my eyes. I try not to think of anything. Just feel. Accept. Believe.

I must have dozed off for a while because the moon is further in its trajectory across the sky when I open my eyes. The stars are glowing brightly overhead, and I try to make out different constellations. What if The Field really is what the Chinese call 'Chi'—the energy that is in everything? Every leaf, every cricket, bird, and rock—every human and every star would all be connected. What's that saying some religions have? "Let go and let God?" Maybe this is sort of the same thing. I need to let the energy of the universe work through me. Stop trying and let it happen. Simple, right?

Not.

The stars seem to be getting brighter and coming closer. Then they begin falling from the sky, raining all around me, bright silver raindrops, like drops of liquid mercury, disappearing into the water, softly striking the surface of the stargazing rock, erupting in a flash and then absorbing into the rock. I reach out my arm to touch them, and they feel like puffs of smoke landing on my hand. I watch the silver shower for a long time. The silent rain envelops the lake, muffling the forest sounds. When the silver drops begin to slow down and then stop altogether, I'm left wondering if it was real or something I created in my imagination. I climb slowly down the rock, still under the spell of the rain.

23

THE TEAM BUS left Monroe High School after lunch on Saturday to drive us to Krueger Stadium in Indianapolis for the championship game. In the parking lot before we boarded the bus, Coach Swenson pulled me and Brett aside.

"We're going with Horton to start today," he says bluntly. My stomach leaps with excitement and settles into a dull ache. He puts a hand on Brett's shoulder. Brett's face is a mask of disappointment. "You played well in last week's game, Brett, but Eric has really stepped it up in practice and shown that he's 100 percent ready."

After Coach leaves, Brett takes a gulp of air, turns to me, and says, "Congratulations. You'll play great."

"Thanks—I'm sorry. You're a great keeper, too." He just nods. Small consolation when he probably won't get to play at all.

When we get there, the girls' final game is still underway, so we watch it for about half an hour and then go to warm up.

Brett's warming me up by sending easy shots for me to save. I parry shots to the right, to the left—punch, catch, dive. Going through the familiar warm-up drills helps a little to settle my nerves and get my head in the game, but there's no denying that this game's different. And I'm still trying to reconcile the fact that I'm starting. In the state championship game. Now the field players take turns taking shots on goal, and Brett takes a turn to give me a break. I get my water bottle from the side of the goal and take a long drink. My breath comes out like puffs of smoke in the cool evening air.

The girls' game is almost over—ten minutes left. After a few rounds of shots on goal, Coach calls us over for the pre-game talk and then we walk over to the stands to watch them award the trophy to the winning girls' team. No one's talking much. We're all trying to stay focused and calm.

Mom and Dad, Drew and his friends, and Marcie and her friend Sara, arrive as the girls' awards ceremony is ending. Drew runs over to me.

"Eric! Are you starting?" he calls out as he crashes into me.

"Hey, buddy," I say, "Yes, I am," and I hold out my hand for a fist bump.

"You're going to win tonight, I know it!" Drew exclaims with the confidence of an eight-year-old.

"Thanks, I hope you're right." I don't really want to do any small talk, so I just wave to my parents.

"Good luck!" my mom calls to me, but they don't come over. I think they realize that I need to focus.

When the field is clear, we make our way over to our bench. Only ten minutes till game time. I see Renee with Bonnie and Cole paying to get in. She catches my eye and mouths something to me. I think it was *Fly*. I smile inwardly. Sometimes it feels that way when I'm diving for the ball. Like I can fly. I wave to her and then line up with my team and walk onto the field.

It's a bit surreal, standing, facing the crowd and waving when the announcer calls out my name. I smile and acknowledge the cheers, but it feels like I'm in a bubble of quiet, and it's all happening around me. My focus is on what comes next. It's *game time*.

A few minutes after play gets underway, Tyler sends a ball back to me. It's a good way for me to get my first touch of the game, and he knows it. Easy and routine. I stop the ball and then send it long to the left wing. *Bam!* My foot connects solidly with the ball. A feeling of calm comes over me and I take a deep breath. I focus my thoughts on the game and anticipating where the play is moving. I'm staying loose in the goal and bouncing on my toes to keep my muscles warm and ready. The ball could come my way any time.

It's another physical game with Fort Ben, like the last one, but this time the refs are calling the fouls, which keeps it under control. We're getting a lot of shots on goal, and the other keeper is getting frustrated with his team. He makes a save and then takes the punt, but he shanks it and it only goes to midfield.

The Fort Ben midfielder takes the ball from around the center stripe and makes a solo run toward our goal. My defenders are in good shape, ready to challenge him. I'm watching and ready, covering the goal. He passes it right to the wing, who carries it a few yards and then crosses the ball into a crowd of players arriving in front of the goal. I see it like it's happening in slow motion. The ball comes sailing through the air from my right. Fort Ben's striker is running on to it; Will is there to cover him. They both go up for the header, but I can't see clearly because Raul is shielding me.

Without a conscious decision, I reach out my left hand where I know the ball is coming, and *smack!*—it hits my palm and ricochets into the air. It hurts, but not enough to distract me. I keep my eyes on the ball and lunge forward into the crowd, shoving through players, grab the ball out of the air, and pull it into my chest.

"YES!" I yell out and pump my fist in the air. This is as much to psych out the other team as it is to pump myself up, but this time it means even more because *I knew where the ball was going to be.* The flash of insight is back. *About time.*

I take the punt, powering it downfield into the opposite penalty box. That feeling of energy or adrenaline is zinging through me so that I feel like I could lift the goal and throw it across the field or sprint down the field in five leaps.

In the thirty-sixth minute, Paul takes the ball down the sideline, jukes past two defenders, and sends a pass to the top of the box, where Dameon runs onto it, wide open because the defender has drifted over toward Paul. Dameon connects with his left foot and buries a shot into the lower right corner. Monroe scores! *Up one!*

Dameon runs to the sideline by the stands and slides on his knees in the grass in front of the fans. The rest of the team piles on top of him.

Our euphoria is short lived, because instead of feeling defeated, Fort Ben is fueled by their desire to win. Taking control of the ball from the kickoff, they make two decisive passes downfield, moving toward me and evading my defenders. The Fort Ben striker gets control of the ball and takes a point blank shot from ten yards out. I'm off my feet before he takes the shot, but not quite fast enough. The ball screams past my fingertips before plowing into the net in the back of the goal. It was a good goal. Not much I could do about it. I was fully extended and anticipated the shot, but I can't save every one. Not against a team like Fort Ben. But it still sucks.

It's tied 1–1 at halftime. Everyone can taste victory, but we still have to make it happen. I'm totally jazzed because I feel like I'm back in the zone, with The Field or whatever it is, but the game's not over yet. Anything can happen. The second half is a battle between equally matched teams—great for the fans to watch, but a bitch to play. By the seventy-third minute, the field players have all probably run six miles each, and I've hit the ground more times than I can remember. The pressure's on now. We've got to score in the next seven minutes, or it goes to overtime, then penalty kicks. No one wants a championship game decided with penalty kicks.

Paul, Raul, and Dameon are taking shots, but nothing's going in. Dameon's shot goes over the goal. It looks like Paul's is going in—but it slams into the crossbar, ricochets off, and a Fort Ben player clears it. The ball comes to my end of the field, and I make an easy save and punt the ball to where Paul is positioned on the left side. He takes the ball and starts dribbling downfield toward the Fort Ben goal. He doesn't pass, which is dangerous, because it makes you a target for the other team to take the ball from you, but it's what every fan thinks of—the amazing runs of Messi or Maradona, evading player after player, and then scoring the winning goal. But that's exactly what Paul does. He puts everything he's got into this run, all the footwork, all the speed, and when he gets within striking distance, he sends a rocket into the upper ninety. *Score!* Two to one.

The clock keeps running, and now there are only three minutes left in regular time. Fort Ben can see their championship title slipping away. It's now or never, so they come out with everyone focused on scoring. Even their keeper has moved out of the box. We've got everyone back on D. The seconds tick by, but Fort Ben can't get a shot off. I'm waiting and watching, because I know a shot is coming. I try to calm my mind and feel it, not think it, not force it. Then, with thirty seconds left, it happens. The striker gets the ball and takes his shot. He shoots it from twenty-five yards out, right at the goal, the trajectory going over my head. It's one of those shots that could go over the goal, or just slip in right under the crossbar and are wickedly hard to save because you have to dive backward. Again, it feels like slow motion. I wait, coiled, until it's just the right moment, and then—*Now!*

I launch myself into the air, extending my arm toward the sky, reaching back and up to the crossbar, eight feet in the air. It's like I'm propelled by some invisible force that's merged with my body. I'm fully extended, arched over backward with my hand reaching toward the sky. The ball descends, and I get my palm to it at just the last instant, tipping it backward over the goal, where it rolls along the netting and falls into the grass. I land heavily, flat out on my back, slumped on the grass inside the goal. Before I can even catch my breath, the rest of the team is on top of me and I hear, muffled through the bodies, the buzzer sounding out the end of the match. *We won.*

The team is going crazy; parents and students are screaming in the stands. Paul is pounding me on the back. The other players lift me and Paul onto their shoulders and carry us over in front of the stands and then over to the benches, where they put us down so they can dump the big cooler of water on Coach Swenson and then they carry him across the field. I'm yelling as loud as anyone else. We won the state championship. Unbelievable. Awesomely unbelievable. *We are state champions!*

The awards ceremony is just a blur. One by one they announce the names of all the Monroe players, and everyone cheers. When they present the trophy to Coach Swenson, he holds it high over his head. By the end of the evening my face hurts from smiling.

Even though we're all spent, no one sleeps on the bus ride home. Everyone's hyped up from the win, especially Will.

"I got a text that there's a party tonight at Trip Vickery's house," he says to me and Paul and Tyler. "Everyone's gonna be there celebrating the win. We've gotta go."

I can't say that I mind the idea of basking in the glory of winning. "Sounds cool. I'll text Renee to see if she wants to meet me there."

We rehash the game on the ride home, going over every play and call. For most of us it's just the end of the season, and it couldn't have ended in a better way, but for the seniors it's the end of their high school careers. Most of them probably aren't thinking about that now, except for maybe Brett. He's celebrating along with everyone else, but it has to be somewhat of a downer for him to end high school without having played much in the tournament. Even though breaking my fingers sucked, I'm kind of glad it gave him a chance to play in semistate. As long as I got to play in the final.

24

THE VICKERYS LIVE outside of town on about thirty-five acres. At one time it was probably all farmland and pastures, but now they just use it for fun. There's a race track for go-carts, a nine hole golf course with a stream running through it, and a small lake. By the time I get there, dozens of cars line the long drive back to the barn. I should be feeling totally stoked about tonight's win, and I do, but there's also something else bugging me at the back of my mind that's making me on edge, apprehensive.

I park at the end of the line, a few cars back from Will's Taurus. When we got off the bus at school, he didn't ask me if I wanted to go with him. No surprise there.

The barn is a great place for a party since they only use it for storage and there isn't much that can get broken. And it's huge. The double doors are open wide, and I can see the cavernous space filled with what looks like half the school milling around under the rafters two stories above. Haylofts no longer full of hay are located high at either end, but the rest is a wide-open space. I think they might even use it as a basketball court in the winter time. Outside in the yard a bonfire is blazing, and groups of people are standing around and sitting on hay bales close to its warmth. As I approach the clumps of students, some of them recognize me and break away.

"Eric!" A guy that I know from Calc class gives me a high five. "You're the man! Awesome save there at the end. Congrats on the championship!"

"Thanks, man," I say and slap his hand. Then I see Bonnie and Cole by the bonfire and head their way. They're deep in conversation when I walk up to them. "Have you guys seen Renee? She's not answering my texts."

"She got here a while ago with her artsy friends. I think they went into the barn." Cole makes quotes in the air with his fingers when he says "artsy." "But I haven't seen her recently. Fantastic game tonight, dude. You and Paul really made it happen."

"Yeah, thanks. It's a team effort, totally," I say reflexively and then I look at Bonnie and add, "Will played great defense, too." She has an expression on her face that I can't decipher. I'm not sure if she's mad or sad, or both.

"I haven't exactly seen a lot of Will lately," she says. She brings her hands to her mouth and blows on them, shuttering the expression in her eyes with her lashes and closing down her face.

"Join the club," I reply. There's a long silence while the three of us, who used to be the four of us, contemplate the change in Will.

I'm impatient to find Renee, so I tell them that I'm going to look for her in the barn. As I wander through the crowd, talking to people and being congratulated, I have a growing sense of unease. *Where's Renee? Why hasn't she texted me?* I start to shrug it off, but then I think—*Trust your gut. Something's wrong.* The skin on my arms and the back of my neck is crawling, and I feel an urgent need to find her. I push past a group of girls and see Anna and

Emily standing by the food table. I rush up to Emily and grab her by the arms.

"Hey!" she cries out. "What's your problem?"

"Where's Renee?" I'm breathing heavily. I probably seem like a stalker, but I don't care.

"She and Miles went inside to find a bathroom," Anna says with a dismissive wave of her hand.

"Where inside?"

"Up to the house. On the other side of the hill." She gives me a quizzical look, sensing my anxiety. "But they'll be back any minute if you want to hang out here and wait for them."

"Ah, no, thanks." I turn and move toward the barn doors. *Miles. She's with Miles.*

I can't easily get past the people in the barn, but when I get to the open doors I sprint across the yard toward the low hill on the other side, shadowy in the flickering light from the bonfire. All I can think is that Renee's in some kind of danger and that I need to get to her. Now.

At the top of the hill, I pause and see the house over to the left down a gradual slope. I run down the hill, stumble and catch myself, and then tear across the gravel driveway, pebbles flying from beneath my feet. I pound up the stairs to the porch and the front door, yank on the knob to open it, but it doesn't budge. *Locked. Shit.* I look around for another door, but don't see one, so I leave the porch and jog around the side of the house. There's a small side door next to the garage that opens when I try it. I enter a dimly lit back hallway and there's a hand-printed sign on the far wall that says BATHROOM with an arrow to the right. I rush down the hall, turn, and come to another sign on a closed door—BATHROOM.

It's locked. I shake the handle and pound on the door. "Renee! Are you in there?"

"What the hell?" A guy's voice says from inside. "Hang on a minute." It doesn't sound like Miles. I hear the toilet flush and then the door opens and a guy I know from the football team comes out.

"Can't a guy take a piss in peace?" he says angrily, and then he recognizes me. "Hey, great win tonight," he says and holds out his hand to shake mine. "It's all yours, dude, but there's no Renee in there."

"Have you seen a guy and a girl come in here? Is this the only bathroom?" I shake his hand and run my other hand over my face in frustration.

"I've seen a lot of guys and girls, and I'm sure this isn't the only bathroom," he says, laughing. "Chill out, dude. Go find another chick."

Of course this isn't the only bathroom. I turn away from him and move down the hallway toward the house. *Upstairs.* The sound of the television comes from the family room beyond the kitchen. I walk silently through the dimly lighted kitchen to the doorway at the side of the room, and I find it leads into a dining room and then the entry with a staircase leading up. I take the stairs two at a time. At the landing I stop and listen.

At first I only hear my heart pounding and the blood rushing through my ears. Then I hear her.

"No! Miles, stop!" Not loud, but definitely clear to my ears. *Down the hall to the right.* I see the light under the door.

"Renee!" I grab the knob, and it's locked too. "What're you doing to her? Open the door, you bastard!" I pound the door with both fists.

"Get the hell out of here, Horton. This is none of your business," the little shit yells at me.

"Eric, help me!" Renee calls out, sounding really scared. It's all the invitation I need.

I move to the other side of the hallway and then slam my body into the door. The jamb makes a loud cracking noise, but holds. I try another tack and brace my back against the wall and then kick the door with my punting leg as hard as I can right next to the doorknob. The wood of the door jamb splinters and splits and the door flies open, slamming against the wall. Miles has Renee shoved up onto the sink and is standing between her legs with his pants undone and his hands up her shirt. She's trying to shove him away and is pulling at his hair, but it's not having any effect. When he sees all six foot two inches of me in the doorway practically breathing fire, his eyes go wide and he frantically tries to do up his pants. But it's the relief in Renee's eyes that I'm focused on.

"You sonofabitch," I say in a low voice as I advance on him. He backs away, but I grab the front of his shirt with both hands and shove him back against the wall, lifting him off the ground to look him in the eye. "She said no, and no means no." I slam him harder against the wall, and the back of his head connects with a thud.

"I thought she wanted it too." He's pathetic.

"I should beat you to a pulp. What don't you understand about 'no' and 'stop'?"

Renee grabs my arm and I look down at her, the cloud of anger leaving my eyes. "Eric, don't hit him. That'll just make it worse. It'll be worse for you. He's not worth it," she pleads with me.

Anything for you.

"OK, for you I won't beat the crap out of him, even though he deserves it." My anger dissipates as I let him slide down the wall and crumple to the floor. "If I ever hear that you've harassed another girl, I will come looking for you. Depend on it," I say and punch him in the gut. He doubles over but has enough sense to grab his pants and get out of there as fast as he can.

I turn to Renee and cup her face between my hands. "Are you OK? Did he hurt you? I'm sorry I didn't get here sooner." I pull her to me and wrap my arms around her. She buries her face in my shoulder and starts to cry.

"No, I'm OK. I'm sorry—you were right," she gulps out between sobs. "I thought you were just jealous of Miles. I thought he was harmless. I always thought if I got into a bad situation I could defend myself, get myself out of it, but I was wrong. He totally overpowered me and there was nothing I could do. It was like I wasn't doing a thing. I was so scared. And then you came." She stops crying and looks up at me. "You knew, didn't you?"

I brush her hair off her forehead and kiss her eyelids, tasting her salty tears. "I'm glad you're OK." I pause and take a deep breath. "He just always gave me a bad feeling and tonight . . . When I found out you were with Miles . . . I can't explain it, but I'm glad I paid attention."

"So am I. Thank you." When I start to open my mouth to speak, she puts her finger to my lips to silence me. "You should always pay attention to those feelings. I was wrong when I said they aren't real." She moves her finger and kisses me, which also has the effect of silencing me.

We stand together for several minutes while Renee collects herself. I run my hand down the back of her head, stroking her hair, not sure of the best way to comfort her. I'm so relieved that she's OK, but for some reason I still have a sense of unease. Like a low undercurrent of foreboding. I want to shake it off, but I can't.

Renee rinses off her tear-stained face and fixes her makeup at the sink. She turns to me and asks, "Do I look OK? Are my eyes puffy?" She's a little pink around her nose and her eyes are especially green, and maybe a little puffy, but I think she looks beautiful.

"You look perfect," I say. "You're beautiful." I put my arm around her and kiss the top of her head. "Do you feel like staying or do you want me to take you home?"

"No. Let's stay and have fun. I don't want to let Miles ruin the night." We quietly make our way downstairs and walk back across the hill toward the barn.

"Let's stay outside by the bonfire," Renee says. Cole and Bonnie are still there, but they've moved to sit on one of the hay bales. Some of the guys from the team are also there, enjoying the attention from the other kids. We go over to talk to Cole and Bonnie.

"I see you found her," Cole remarks.

"Yeah, I did." I have my arm around Renee's waist, and she's staying pretty close by my side.

"We have marshmallows and sticks if you want to roast them in the fire." Bonnie picks up a bag of marshmallows from one of the hay bales. "There might still be some chocolate and graham crackers on the table over there if you want to make s'mores."

"So what's been going on?"

"You're seeing it. Everyone's hanging out and celebrating the big win. The soccer players are all rock stars now, as you're probably aware. Will's been especially enjoying the attention," he says sarcastically.

"Yeah, well, he deserves it. He played great D tonight—all season really." Sometimes Cole's snarkiness can get irritating. He's always trying to shoot somebody down.

"There's also beer stashed in the woods and a bunch of people have been going over there and coming back really happy, if you know what I mean."

"Will's the 'happiest' one of them all," Bonnie chimes in. "He's being really loud and obnoxious."

"I guess he's just having a good time. I mean, he's not really hurting anyone, right? And we did just win the championship." I'm not sure why I'm defending him, except that it seems like someone needs to take his side.

"He's just been acting really stupid lately," Bonnie says quietly. I can't argue with that, because it's totally true.

We hang out with Cole and Bonnie until it gets late. Renee makes us each two s'mores, and she and Bonnie sit together talking intently about whatever it is girls talk about.

Behind them I see Paul coming purposely toward us.

"Have you guys seen Asplunth? He's totally wasted and out of control," Paul says when he reaches the group. "I think we should do something."

"Like what?" Cole shrugs.

"I don't know. Take his keys or something." Paul runs a hand through his black hair—as a senior, he didn't have to shave his head for the tournament. Will and I refused to shave ours even though we're juniors. "Did he drive?" he asks.

"Yeah, he did," I say. "I saw his car when I came in." The undercurrent of foreboding swells into a tight knot in the pit of my stomach.

"That's not good," Paul says. "He shouldn't drive. He's wasted."

As if on cue, we hear a loud commotion on the other side of the yard by the driveway. Will is there with his new buddies. We can't really hear what they're saying, but one thing is clear. Will has his car keys in his hand.

"Shit," says Paul. "We've got to stop him."

"Let's go. I'll try to drive him home. Renee can take my car." We gather up our stuff and follow Will as fast as we can. He's already out of sight down the driveway. By the time we catch up with him, he's gotten into his car and started the ignition. I knock on the window to get his attention.

"Hey, was'up dude?" he says when he rolls down the window. His smile is crooked and his words are definitely slurred.

"Why don't you let me drive you home? You're drunk. You shouldn't be driving," I say.

His smile disappears. "No. I'm fine. I'm not going home, anyway. There's another party over at Steve McMahon's house that we're all going to."

"I'll go with you. Move over and let me drive." I move to open the door, but he's already got his hand on the automatic door lock and I hear a click before I can pull the handle.

"I said no." He jams the car into gear, revving past me out of his spot and doing a U-turn in the drive around us. Paul yells and tries to stop him by getting in front of the car, but Will just veers around him onto the grass and takes off fast down the driveway, spraying gravel from his tires.

"Crap—what should we do now?" Paul asks. "Call the cops?"

"Let's follow him. We can try to get him to pull over. My car's right here." I'm already moving toward the van and unlocking the doors with the remote. Now that uneasy feeling has turned into full-fledged fear. "Come on, I don't want to lose him." We all pile in, Renee sitting in the front next to me and Paul behind me, leaning over the back of my seat. Bonnie and Cole squeeze into the back together. I do a quick U-turn and follow Will down the drive. He has a pretty good head start on us, and I just see his taillights flash red briefly as he brakes before making a left onto the road.

Once I get to the road, I try to make up the distance between the cars. Will's driving erratically and weaving all over the road.

The Vickery's place is out in the country and it's really late, so fortunately there aren't any other cars on the road. We get to within a few car lengths of the Taurus—I don't want to get any closer. I start honking the horn at him and flashing my brights. He speeds up. Not the response I was hoping for.

"Man, this is crazy," Paul says over my shoulder. "I don't think this is such a good idea."

"Be careful," Renee cautions as I speed up to keep pace with him. I look over at her and see that her knuckles are white from gripping the arm rest so tightly.

Will turns onto the road that goes past the lagoons. He takes the corner so fast that his car fishtails before straightening out on the road. I see the headlights of another car approaching. Not good. My heart is pounding. How can we get him to stop? He's acting totally irrational. Maybe we shouldn't have chased him. But calling the police seemed so extreme, and they'd just chase him, too. Would he have stopped for them?

We see the Taurus go off onto the low shoulder and then jerk back onto the road, but Will's overcompensated and the car careens into the other lane, directly in the path of the oncoming car. Then the Taurus jerks to the right, missing the other car, but this time it goes completely off the road and into the field. It appears to be totally out of control, careening and bumping across the uneven ground and heading straight for a huge tree directly in his path.

"Oh my God!" Bonnie screams from the back seat.

"No!" yells Renee. She's leaning forward in her seat and Paul has my shoulder in a vice grip. I skid over to the side of the road and jerk to a stop. We watch in horror, helpless as Will's car speeds closer to the tree for what looks like a head-on collision, and then at the very last minute the car jerks to the right, skidding away. The front end narrowly misses the tree, but the back end on the driver's side swings around, slamming the side of the car into the trunk with a sickening crunching sound that jolts it abruptly to a stop.

We're all out of the car and running toward the crash. I hear Cole on his cell calling 9-1-1.

Steam and smoke are pouring from the hood of the car when I get there. I try to yank open the front passenger side door, but it's still locked.

"Find a rock or something to break the window!" I yell. Through the window I see Will slumped over the airbag, apparently unconscious. The white material of the airbag is smeared with blood. The driver's side door is smashed up against the tree, pinning him in.

"Here!" Renee runs toward me with a grapefruit-sized rock. "Hurry, I smell gasoline." I meet her eyes and I see the fear there.

Realization hits me. "My dreams," I say. "The explosions." Dread constricts my chest. This can't be happening.

"Yes," she says, nodding. "Hurry."

I take the rock from her, step back, lift it high over my head, and launch it at the window. The safety glass shatters, sending a thousand sharp missiles showering over us. Reaching through the jagged hole, I unlock the door and pull it open.

"Can you get him out?" Paul yells.

"I don't know." I crawl onto the bucket seat of the Taurus and see that Will's chest is rising and falling. *At least he's not dead,* I think, but I can't tell how badly he's hurt. The blood on the airbag is coming from a gash on his forehead. Amazingly, he's wearing his seatbelt. He's wedged between the airbag, the seat, and the driver's side door, which is pressed up against the left side of his body from where it collided with the tree.

I don't want to hurt him any more than he already is, but I know with certainty that I have to get him out of the car before it explodes. The smell of gasoline is getting stronger, and the seconds are ticking away. I'm not really thinking, just going on autopilot, doing the next thing that needs to be done, pushing back the panic.

I unlatch his seat belt and kneel half on the seat, half on the center console. Hooking my left arm over his shoulder and under his left armpit and my right hand under his right arm, I try to pull him toward me. At first he seems to be coming free, but then I feel resistance and he starts to groan. I'm afraid to pull too hard and can't really see the lower part of his body, but I think his left leg is stuck where the car is smashed in, pinning him inside.

"I think he's stuck!" I yell over my shoulder to Paul, who's practically on top of me in the door of the car.

I pull harder, trying to see if I can somehow free Will's leg, but he groans louder, his eyes flickering open and then rolling back in his head, and I can't get him loose. "This isn't working. We have to try something else." I just haven't figured out what.

"I'm coming out," I tell Paul, who moves out of the way, and I scramble out backward after him. Cole, Bonnie, and Renee are huddled together to one side. There's a middle-aged guy standing behind Paul who must be the driver of the other car that Will almost hit.

"His leg is stuck on the other side of the car where it's smashed against the tree," I tell them. "I can't pull him out from this side. We need to free his leg first."

"How? How're we going to do that?" Paul is wild-eyed and his hair is standing on end from where he's been running his hands through it.

"We have to move the car away from the tree," I say calmly and with what I hope is authority. An idea is forming in my mind. From the moment I started running across the field toward Will's car, I could feel the energy from the stargazing rock and the power from the earth and the ley lines coursing through me. As the urgency of the situation heightened, the feeling's been growing stronger. I think I might be able to channel the power of The Field to get Will free of the car. I at least have to try.

"Are you nuts? How're we going to do that?" Paul demands.

"I've heard about people doing stuff like that, you know, in an emergency," Bonnie says, stepping forward. "It's like they get superhuman strength or something."

"The Field," says Renee, coming over to me and putting her hand on my arm. "Do you feel it?" I nod and she adds, "We're by the lagoons. It must be really strong here. I think I can feel something, too."

"What the hell are you talking about?" says Paul. "We need to do something! Where are the paramedics? They should be here by now." It feels like an eternity since the crash, but it's really only been one or two minutes.

"Come on," I say and move quickly to the rear of the car. "Everyone grab hold of the bumper. We're going to lift it up and move it away from the tree." We all line up behind the trunk. "Put your hands underneath and use your legs to lift." Cole and Paul and the other driver look at me skeptically, but at this point we're desperate to get Will out, so they line up. I position myself in the center between the others. "OK, now just concentrate on lifting the car and moving it on the count of three." I take a deep breath. "Ready? One, two, three—LIFT!"

I use all my strength, pushing up with my legs, focusing my thoughts on accessing the power that I know is there. I feel the car lift up a few inches and move slightly to the right. Not enough. Images from my dreams flash into my mind. Black and orange explosions, red-hot fire, screaming.

"That was good!" I yell. My breath comes out in puffs of steam in the chilly night air, but I'm sweating with the exertion, and I have to wipe my face on my sleeve so I can see past the sweat trickling into my eyes. I grab onto the bumper. "Again on three. We can do this! One, two, three—LIFT!" A deep, primal yell comes welling out of my core, and I lift with everything I've got, feeling the limitless power of the universe flowing through me, giving me strength.

A loud guttural sound bursts out of me, and we lift the car up off the ground and move it several feet to the right before dropping it back to the ground with a crash, where it rocks violently back and forth on its springs.

"We did it! I can't believe it, we actually did it!" Paul yells and runs to the driver's side door, but his excitement quickly fades when he gets there. I'm right behind him and see that the metal of the door is crumpled like aluminum foil and caved in right where Will is sitting. The door frame is bent like a smashed beer can. Through the broken window we can see Will clearly, slumped over the airbag, his shoulder at an odd angle, blood running down his face from multiple cuts. Paul tries the handle, then pulls on the door frame, but it doesn't budge. "Damn it," he says, slamming his hand against the roof. The others are standing close behind us.

"What do we do now?" Bonnie cries.

"I don't know, but we'd better hurry or pray that help gets here soon, because gas is leaking and the fumes could ignite at any minute," the guy from the other car says. I look down and see gasoline pooling in the grass beneath our feet.

"All of you, get way back," I yell. "It's gonna explode." I take off my jacket and put it over the jagged edge of the window to cover the bits of broken glass and sharp pieces of metal sticking out, grab the frame of the door with both hands, and put my right foot against the car for leverage. I'm hardly thinking at all, just acting on pure emotion. Time has slowed down for me, but also expanded so that I see Will through the window and my hands on the door, and I also see the scene as if I'm viewing it from a distance, like a long shot in a movie, with the others huddled together a short distance away and me by the car. I feel both a laser focus and an odd detachment from the scene. All I know is that Will, my best friend, will probably die unless I get this door open.

In my head, I count to three and begin to pull with my arms and push against the car and the earth with my feet. I feel the effort of pulling, but it's not painful or even particularly difficult. Power is flowing to me, through me. It's part of me and I am part of it. I know I can do this. The door starts to move, imperceptibly at first, and then I hear the sound of metal giving way, ripping apart, coming loose. Incredibly, I find that I can pull even harder, and the door abruptly tears free, making me stumble backward from the momentum. I regain my balance and shove it fully open.

Will is slumped over the airbag, his left arm bent at an unnatural angle and his left leg exposed, showing a deep gash in his thigh. I put one arm behind his back and the other under his legs and carefully pull him from the wreckage. His head lolls onto my shoulder as I lift him into my arms, his breath warm on my face. In the distance I hear sirens wailing.

Hurry. The strong smell of gasoline is all around us. I turn away from the car with Will in my arms and run as best I can toward the others. I've only gone about twenty feet when the car explodes.

25

THE FORCE OF the explosion slams into me like a sledge hammer, and I fall to my knees, dropping Will to the ground. The heat is next, searing my back. I cover my head with my arms and hunch my body over Will's to shield him as much as possible. Someone starts screaming.

After the initial explosion, I look back and see red-hot orange and yellow flames engulfing the car, tongues of fire like a living thing lighting up the night and spewing black smoke. Right where Will had been sitting. Right where I was a moment ago. Within a few seconds the others are upon us. Bonnie is crying, tears stream unchecked down her face, streaking it with black mascara. She kneels next to Will where he's sprawled on the ground, still unconscious, and puts her hand on his bloody cheek. Paul is saying, "Oh my God, oh my God," over and over like a mantra, and Cole and the other driver just stand there in shock. Renee kneels down next to me and puts her arm around my shoulders.

"You saved him," she says. I turn to her and lose it. All the energy and adrenaline whooshes out of me and I'm left a spent and ragged shell. I grab on to her like a life raft and bury my head in her shoulder, clutching fistfuls of her hair. She puts her arms around my shaking body and just holds me while I try to pull myself together. The magnitude of what could have happened crashes over me. But it didn't happen. Will is hurt, but he's OK. I lift my head to take in a lungful of cold night air and wipe my face on my sleeve.

"I'm OK," I tell her, which is only partly true. I still feel totally used up and physically unsteady, but I'm calm. The worst is over and I made it through.

The ambulance and fire trucks arrive at almost the same time, sirens wailing and lights pulsing and flashing, dispelling the dark. The paramedics rush toward us and we're happy to let the professionals take over. The firefighters quickly pull out hoses and start dowsing the fiery inferno with torrents of water.

The six of us get out of the way while the paramedics work on Will. One of them comes over and gives us some blankets, and I realize that it's gotten much colder and my teeth are chattering, but it's as much from shock as the cold. Renee and I huddle together under a blanket and numbly watch the paramedics and firefighters work to contain the fire and stabilize Will.

Then the police arrive and we talk to them about what happened and call Will's parents and our own families. I wonder what kind of trouble Will's going to be in—with the police and Coach Swenson—but the officers don't say anything about it. Before the ambulance leaves to take Will to the hospital, Bonnie asks the paramedics if he'll be OK.

"Yes, honey, he's gonna be just fine." The woman paramedic pats her arm and reassures her. "The gashes on his head and leg definitely need stitches, and he may have broken his left arm, but nothing that won't heal."

"SO HOW DID you get him out of the car exactly?" one of firefighters asks me. He and I are standing next to Will's Taurus, now blackened and smoking. Melted paint hangs off the exterior like crêpe-paper streamers, and water drips rhythmically to the already soaked ground. The firefighter has his helmet in his hand and is rubbing his head, puzzled. The interior of the car is a gaping, charred hole. The driver's side door hangs open, and the burnt remains of my jacket cling to the edge of the window. "Because, this looks like something we would usually have to use the Jaws of Life to get open." I've already been through it a couple of times with the police and the fire chief, but patiently I say again, "All of us picked up the back end of the car and moved it away from the tree, and then I wrenched open the door to get to him." Which is what happened, and saying it that way makes it seem almost like a normal everyday occurrence. But he and I both know it isn't.

"I know that's what you did, but I can't quite wrap my head around exactly how you did it. Even when I can see it with my own eyes right here in front of me."

"I don't know how I did it. I can't explain it either." I can't explain to him that I felt a strength and power that I've never felt before in my life. Not on the soccer field and not in Dr. Auberge's lab. At the moment I needed strength, it was there. I didn't consciously do anything except have the need and the desire and a singular focus. The power felt infinite, limitless, enormous. And in the core of my being, it felt good and right. I have no doubt now that there is a Universal Energy Field, and that I am able to access it, that probably we can all access it.

I've already reassured the police that I'm OK enough to drive, and, after we've each given our statements, they tell us we're free to go home. I take Cole and Bonnie and Paul back to the Vickery's to get their cars. No one says much during the drive, but when I stop to let them out, I get out to stretch my legs and each of them gives me a big hug in turn. Paul pounds me on the back and says, "You're the beast." And Bonnie whispers, "Thank you for not giving up on Will."

26

I'm SITTING IN an incredibly uncomfortable orange plastic chair in Will's hospital room the next morning, waiting for him to wake up. He has a white bandage wrapped around his head, and his left arm is encased in a cast from wrist to shoulder and immobilized in a sling. His left leg is lying on top of the blanket, where I can see the bandage on his thigh, and his face is black and blue from the impact of the airbag. He looks like he was in a really bad fight and got his ass kicked. Knowing that he's going to be OK makes me able to wonder if this is the kind of ass-kicking that he needed. Maybe it's not the nicest thing I've ever thought, but I hope it's true. I hope this wakes Will up to how self-destructive he was being.

But the reason I'm here isn't to talk to him about that. Last night, after dropping off Renee, I had to talk to my parents for a while about the accident, and then I totally crashed into bed, exhausted, and fell immediately asleep. At some point in the middle of the night I woke up completely disoriented. I'd been dreaming about Will's dad and being at the coal gasification plant with him and Will. He was giving us a tour and they were arguing, and the entire time I was trying to get his attention to tell him something. I kept saying, "Mr. Asplunth! Mr. Asplunth!" but he didn't hear me and I couldn't tell him that something was terribly wrong. The words were stuck in my throat. Then I couldn't find him or Will, and when I finally did see them, Mr. Asplunth was at the end of a long hallway silhouetted against a backdrop of fire and Will was running toward him yelling "No!" That's when I woke up. I still smelled like smoke from the accident and for a minute after I woke up, I thought I could smell the fire from the dream. It scared me even more than the explosion dreams, because in this dream I could see the people and the place where I knew something terrible was going to happen.

So this morning I'm here because, after having the explosion dreams come true, I'm not about to ignore this dream. Especially since this time there were actual people and a place in the dream. I don't know exactly what I'm going to say to Will, though. It seems pretty clear that it has something to do with the gasification plant and Will's dad. Because of everything that's happened to me, I know there is more out there than we could possibly understand. I'm ready to accept that it's real, but it's a totally different thing to tell someone else, someone like Will, that you had a dream about his dad and a fire at the coal plant and you're here to warn him. So, I'm just sitting here in this uncomfortable chair waiting and hoping that I'll know the right thing to say when Will wakes up.

After a few minutes, the nurse comes in and says she has to check on Will.

"How're you doing, young man?" she says cheerfully to Will as she jostles his shoulder to wake him. She pulls the curtain closed around the bed and does whatever she needs to do, taking his temperature and blood pressure, I guess. Will groans awake and says groggily, "I feel like I've been trampled by a herd of elephants, but otherwise I'm great."

"You're pretty lucky from what I understand," she replies.

"Yeah, I know," he says quietly.

"You have a visitor," the nurse tells him.

"Mom? Are you still here? I thought you were going home to get some sleep."

"No, it's Eric."

"Oh, hey," he says. We can't really talk since the curtain is still closed and the nurse is there, so we're both silent while she chatters to Will about what she's doing. When she's finished she opens the curtain sharply, making the metal hooks rattle and crash against the wall.

When she's gone, I say, "You look like shit." Trying to be funny, to alleviate the seriousness of his being in the hospital covered in bandages.

"Well, that's pretty much how I feel. The drugs they're giving me definitely give you an awesome buzz, but I wouldn't recommend crashing your car to get some." He cracks a smile and then grimaces. "Even my face hurts."

"Your face got slammed by the airbag."

"I don't remember much from last night, which could be a good thing. I do remember you trying to stop me from leaving the party, and losing control of the car and heading for the tree, but nothing after that." He pauses, looks down at his bandaged leg, and smoothes the sheet over his lap. Then he looks up at me directly and says, "My mom told me that you guys moved the car away from the tree and that you pulled me out of the car just before it exploded. That if it weren't for you, I would be toast, literally. The fire trucks wouldn't have gotten there in time. Man, I don't even know what to say." He leans his head back against the pillows. "You saved my life. And I've been such a freaking asshole to you." He looks at me again. "I'm sorry, man." He chokes out the last few words and wipes his hand across his eyes.

"You'd do it for me. Those drugs must really be messing with you, dude." I pull my chair away from the window, closer to the side of the bed.

"Yeah, the drugs definitely do a number on you. I know I was screwing up. I knew it even while I was doing it, but I was so pissed at my dad and the drinking made it all go away, at least for a while. I always woke up feeling like crap the next day, but this is definitely the worst I've felt after a party." He forces out a laugh and tries to smile, then grimaces again. "Shit, that hurts. Everything hurts." He leans back against the pillows. "I wanna know how you did it. How'd you move the car and get the door open? 'Cause my mom told me that the paramedics were talking about it when they brought me in. They couldn't believe you pulled the door off the car with your bare hands."

He's looking at me with a strange detached look, but I'm not sure if that's just because of all the bruises. Instead of the scorn he had started to show when we talked about Dr. Auberge's work, he looks somewhat hopeful now, almost eager. I choose my words carefully, because I want him to really believe me, so that he'll believe me when I tell him about the dream with his dad in it.

"You know how I've been doing the remote viewing stuff with Dr. Auberge and how he's also doing experiments with The Field?" He nods. "Well, I've been working on some experiments to learn how to access The Field with my thoughts." I'm watching Will as I talk, and his expression still has that foggy look about it. He's still listening and he doesn't look angry or anything, so I continue. "When your car crashed into the tree, we all ran over to you, but we couldn't get you out. We were pretty much freaking out at that point because gas was leaking everywhere, so we all just picked up the car and moved it away from the tree. It was really that simple. We just wanted to do it and we did it. But the driver's side door was still jammed shut, and you were trapped inside, so I pulled it open. I know it sounds crazy, but that's what happened. I think we were able to somehow tap into the Universal Energy Field." I so badly want him to believe me. To believe The Field is real. I want to share it with him, talk to him about it.

"Damn. You did that? I didn't really believe any of it, you know. The stuff with Dr. Auberge. But now, I don't know what to think." He's silent for a moment, considering. The fingers of his right hand pluck absently at a loose thread on the sheet. "But how did you do it?" I'm relieved that he isn't scoffing at me, like he was before when he was acting like it was magic or something I made up.

"That's the thing, I don't really know for sure. I just wanted to very badly, and I knew that I could. I also felt something from the stargazing rock, I think. Like extra power or energy or something. It's hard to explain." I sit forward in the orange chair. "There's something else."

"Something even more out there than this?" He raises his eyebrows, but he's listening, so I go on.

"Yeah, I know, but hang with me on this." I take a deep breath and plunge in. "I'd been having dreams about it, about the explosion. Since the beginning of the school year."

"You knew it was going to happen?" he asks, adjusting his injured arm against the bed railing.

"No. I didn't know what the dreams were about. They were just explosions and fire and screaming, but there weren't any people in the dreams or a car or anything. They really freaked me out. When you crashed and the gas was leaking and we were afraid it was going to explode, I knew the dreams were about the crash and we had to get you out before the car exploded."

"That's crazy, man. I mean, that you dreamed about it and it happened. Not that it's actually crazy. And that you were there and could use that energy field." He forgets his cuts and bruises and shakes his head and then groans and puts his right hand on the side of his head. "See, just thinking about it is making my head hurt."

"I had another dream last night."

"I don't think I'd survive another one of your dreams. If it's all the same to you, could you dream about somebody else?"

"It wasn't about you. Well, you were in it, but it was about your dad."

"My dad? He was here last night, but I was too out of it. I didn't see him." He still has the edge to his voice that's been there when he talks about his dad, but it's colored with something else—longing or maybe sadness. Definitely less anger.

"We were at the coal gasification plant. There was a fire and your dad was in some sort of danger." I don't tell him that he was running after his dad, calling for him with fear and anguish in his voice. I'm not sure how he would take that.

"What kind of danger?"

"The problem is, I don't really know. What I do know is the other dreams came true, and I'm afraid this one could too. You've got to tell your dad. Tell him there's something wrong at the plant. Maybe he can figure out what it is and stop it or fix it."

"So I'm supposed to tell him that you had a dream about a fire at the plant and that he's in some sort of undefined danger, so he needs to look into what it could be? You realize that I haven't even talked to my dad for almost three months?" He's not exactly being sarcastic, but he's not buying it, either.

"That's why he'll listen to you. You said he's been calling and texting you and he wants to talk to you. I think if you asked him, he'd do it. Even though he's been a dick, he still loves you." As soon as the words are out of my mouth, I wish I could take them back. Will looks like I just punched him. His shoulders hunch over and his eyes shut tight. I think I've gone too far, said the wrong thing.

Then he takes a deep breath and lets it out slowly, still with his eyes closed, and says very quietly, so I can barely hear him, "That's the thing, isn't it? Does he?" The pain in his voice is palpable, worse than his physical pain.

I reach over the bed rail and put my hand on his shoulder. "Yes. That's one thing I do know. He totally loves you. He always has, and I know that hasn't changed."

I let go of his shoulder, and we just sit there for a while. After a few minutes, Will's breathing becomes more regular and then his head rolls to the side. He's fallen asleep. As I'm prying myself out of the plastic chair, the door opens and Mr. Asplunth comes in. He stops when he sees me and glances over at the bed and sees that Will's sleeping.

"Eric." He comes the rest of the way into the room and around the foot of the bed to where I'm standing. He holds out his hand to me and says, "Thank you. Thank you for saving my son," but his voice cracks and instead of just shaking my hand he pulls me into a rough embrace.

When I leave, Mr. Asplunth is sitting in the orange chair I just vacated, watching Will and waiting for him to wake up. I'm not going to tell him about the dream. It just seems like something Will should tell him. I hope he'll listen.

27

"SO YOU FELT something from the stargazing rock?" Marcie asks. "It's on the world energy grid, on the ley lines."

"I'm just glad Will is OK," Mom says. "Why didn't you tell us he was drinking to cope with his parents' break up?"

"I guess I should have told you he was doing all this crazy shit."

"Watch your language, please," my dad says sternly.

"Sorry," I say. "And, yeah, I definitely felt something from the stargazing rock. It's hard to describe, but it made me feel, somehow, more. More connected, more aware and powerful. I felt like all the goodness out there was funneling through me, helping me move the car and pull open the door. I know it sounds weird, but that's what it was like."

It's after dinner and we're all still sitting at the table eating ice cream, and the conversation has turned to the crash last night. Renee says, "I felt it too. It seemed like the air was almost crackling with energy. Everything was enhanced, magnified." I nod in agreement.

"God wanted you to help Will," Drew says matter of factly. "That's why the crash was there by the lagoons and the stargazing rock. So you could use the energy and get God's help." Ralph is sitting next to Drew, hoping that he'll slip him some food. Drew has his hand on Ralph's head. Both of them have these goofy smiles on their faces, and yes, Ralph does smile. We all just look at Drew for a long moment, each of us trying to take in what he's just said.

Eventually, my dad says, "Drew, I think you're exactly right."

Drew slips Ralph a piece of chicken left over from dinner, says, "I know," and goes back to eating his chocolate ice cream.

THAT NIGHT, AS I'm getting ready for bed, I get a text from Will: TOLD MY DAD ABOUT UR DREAM AND HE PROMISED TO CHECK IT OUT. WE TALKED FOR A LONG TIME. IT WAS GOOD. I wonder about good things happening as a result of really terrible things, and I fall asleep feeling happy that Will and I are talking again and that Will and his dad are talking again, too.

MY CRAPPY LOCKER is stuck, as usual. I spin the dial in frustration and then slowly and precisely dial the combination and lift the lock. Thankfully, it slips open and I shove my backpack inside and grab my AP Enviro notebook. Today is one of those fantastic fall days when the sun is shining and the temperature is predicted to get up around seventy degrees. Everyone's wearing shorts and T-shirts, although that's not too much of a change for some of the kids. I've seen guys wearing shorts and flip-flops in a snow storm. As usual, the hallways are crowded with students on their way to first period. The sound of their voices bounces off the metal lockers and concrete walls and is amplified into a raucous din. Everyone's talking about the accident and Will, and on my way in people keep asking me if he's all right and wanting me to tell them what happened. The stories I'm hearing are even wilder than the truth. One girl heard that the car hit the tree and rolled three times and that I lifted the car off the ground and flipped it back over. I guess, when you think about it, that isn't much more incredible than what we actually did.

Paul comes up next to me as I'm closing my locker. "Hey," he says, bouncing back and forth from one foot to the other. "Has anyone said anything to you about us winning state? I mean, the crash was a big deal and everything, but nobody's talking about our win! It sucks." He's always full of pent-up energy, and he's literally bouncing around as he talks.

"Don't worry, Coach sent out an email. They're going to say something about it in the morning announcements, and tomorrow's gonna be a spirit day. We're supposed to wear our jerseys."

"Oh, that's cool." He runs his hand through his hair, which seems to settle his jitteriness. "Gotta get to class. See you at lunch."

"Later." I join the flow of students and start making my way across the building. Cole catches up with me just as I get to the doorway of AP Enviro. Today he is wearing a Sesame Street T-shirt with Big Bird and Snuffleupagus on it.

"Are you Big Bird or Snuffleupagus?" I ask.

"Neither," he replies. "I'm Oscar, of course."

"Of course you are," I say and smile to myself. I've always thought Oscar was really a nice guy deep down. Just like Cole. I sit in my usual spot behind Renee, and he heads to the back of the room.

"Hey, babe," I whisper into her ear as I slide into my seat. She turns her head and smiles at me and says, "Hey yourself." My heart zings. All the uneasiness that had been between us is gone. We did a lot of talking over the weekend and worked through stuff, and things are really good between us now. We did a lot of making out, too, which didn't hurt.

The second bell rings, and Mr. Ogle stands in the front of the classroom.

"OK, settle down everyone. Let's get started." He picks up some papers from his desk. "First, I have an announcement to make. Dr. Auberge has selected the student who will fill the internship position in his lab for next semester." Half the class turns to look at me. I try to keep my face blank. "He couldn't be here today to tell you himself, as he is giving a presentation at the International Conference on Nuclear Physics in Trieste, Italy this week. He asked me to tell you that it was a difficult decision to make. All the applications he received showed great talent and interest, but he could only offer one internship. I'm pleased to say that Randy Chin has been selected for the position. Congratulations, Randy."

He begins clapping, and the students start clapping even as they glance back and forth between me and Randy, looking to see my reaction. I clap for him too and keep my expression happy. Randy is looking really excited, and I'm glad for him. I already knew that I wouldn't be getting the internship. Dr. Auberge told me yesterday when I picked up Renee. He said that he didn't want it to appear as favoritism since I was dating Renee and I was already working with him. He wanted to give someone else an opportunity, too. Instead of working in my favor, being Renee's boyfriend actually worked against me. I'd be lying if I said I wasn't disappointed, but it is true that I'll still be working with him and Stephen on experiments with The Field, so I can hardly complain.

Will isn't in school today, but he's home from the hospital, so I told him I'd pick up his assignments. Mr. Ogle is cool and asks me to tell Will that he's glad he's OK, but some of his other teachers won't give the assignments to me because Will hasn't been absent for two days yet. I guess those are the rules and it's more work for them, but you'd think they'd be glad that a student wanted to do the work.

When school's over, I go to the art classrooms to look for Renee so we can go to Will's together.

The smell hits me as soon as I push through the double doors into the art hallway. It's a mixture of wet clay, paint, and turpentine mingled with raw wood and sawdust. Renee is in the same room where I found her the last time, and she calls me over to see the painting she's working on.

"See? I just finished it today. My mother's garden in France." She steps aside so I can have a look.

It's a riot of color and form and at first I can't make sense of it, but then it composes itself into clumps of fruit and vegetables and flowers all jumbled together. I can see why the style is called Impressionism, because I get the impression of the overall picture rather than distinct individual subjects.

"I really like it. Your mother will love it." I put my arm around her shoulders and pull her to me. It feels so good to be in sync with her again. She gives my waist a little squeeze and kisses me lightly on the cheek.

"Just give me a minute to clean up, and I'll be ready." I wander around the room looking at the other paintings while she washes her brushes and puts her paints away. None of the other paintings seem as good as Renee's, but I don't have a clue about what's considered good, and I'm probably biased. I jingle the car keys in my pocket.

We drive with the windows down, enjoying the Indian summer weather. Most of the leaves have already fallen, but there are still a few maples covered in brilliant red or gold leaves, and kids are out everywhere, playing ball, jumping in the leaves and riding bikes. When we get to Will's house, his mom answers the door and takes us back to the family room. She looks a little tired, but not haggard like she did at first after Will's dad left. Even so, Will's accident couldn't have helped with her stress level.

Will is reclining on the sofa with the remote in one hand, surrounded by glasses and plates of half-eaten food.

"Hey, how're you doing?" Renee and I sit down on the love seat opposite the sofa.

"Not bad, considering. The pain is manageable—I'm down to one pill every six hours, and I think I might be able to switch to ibuprofen tomorrow or the next day. The doctor said I can go back to school when I'm off the pain meds."

"You don't look as bad as you did Saturday. Your bruises are yellow and green, not black and blue. Your face isn't all puffy, but you still look like hell. No more pretty boy for a while," I say. "Why do you want to get back to school so bad, anyway? I would've thought you'd want to take it easy."

"I don't know how much time you've spent at home on a weekday, but daytime TV pretty much sucks. It's all soap operas, cooking shows, and home improvement. It's not like we have the soccer channel, either. I figure by the end of the week I'll be bored out of my mind."

"How will you get around school?" Renee asks. "Can you use crutches with your arm?"

"That's the other thing. I'm going to have to use a wheel chair for a while, so I'll need some help."

"I'm sure people will be lining up to push your wheelchair," Renee says, smiling. "You're the talk of the school." Will has the grace to look sheepish.

"Yeah, but not in a good way," he says. "Anyway, did you bring me my homework?" He looks at me and I hand him the folder of papers I brought. "I've got a lot of catching up to do. I was really slacking off before." In a serious tone he says, "This whole thing really scared the shit out of me, you know? Waking up in the hospital, covered in bandages and realizing that I almost died—man, talk about a reality check. I don't want to be that guy. The guy that royally screws up and loses everything." Renee nods. *He almost was that guy.*

"I've got some other news," I say. "Ogle announced in class today who was selected for the internship. Neither of us got it. Dr. Auberge picked Randy Chin."

"You're kidding? I never really thought I would get it, but I was pretty sure you would. That sucks. Do you know why?"

"Yeah, it's actually OK." I glance at Renee and she reaches over and squeezes my hand. "I guess being the boyfriend didn't work in my favor after all." I shrug.

"Oh, yeah, like it sucks to be you," Will says.

"I'll take this over the internship anytime." I look at Renee.

Will's phone rings and he checks the caller ID. "It's my dad." He answers the call. "Hey," he says.

"So you did a check? . . . Really? It could have exploded . . . ?" He takes a sharp intake of breath and turns away from me and Renee. "Yeah, I'm really glad, Dad. Glad you're OK." His voice is muffled now. "I'll tell him." And then, even more quietly, "I love you too." He puts down the phone, and I see his shoulders rise and fall a few moments before he turns to us.

"You won't believe what happened." He leans back against the couch. "My dad decided to have a plant-wide safety check because of what I told him about your dream. They were right in the middle of the check when they noticed some high readings from the furnace. The thing is, the meter wasn't reading properly, or they would already have found it. If they hadn't been doing the safety check, it would have gotten to critical levels. They shut the operation down to check it out. You know what they found? Almost complete blockage of the exhaust stack. If they hadn't found it when they did, the heat and pressure would have built up and caused an explosion. A lot of people could have been injured or killed. Maybe even my dad." Will's hands are tightly gripping the legs of his Monroe Varsity soccer warm-ups. "He said to tell you thanks for the heads-up. However you knew about it."

I have mixed feelings hearing this. On the one hand, I'm glad I was able to prevent something because of my dream, but I also feel the weight of responsibility. How am I supposed to tell what's important and what isn't? I didn't know what the first dreams were about. If I had, could I have prevented Will's accident somehow? What if I miss something and someone gets hurt?

Will is still talking. "What's really incredible is that I don't think my dad believed me when I told him about your dream. I think the only reason he even did the safety check was because he was so glad we were talking again and he wanted to keep it going." He pauses for a moment, considering. "If I hadn't had the accident and gotten a total reality check . . . I wouldn't have been able to tell him about your dream. I wouldn't even have been talking to him."

"It got the two of you talking again," Renee says. "Your dad did the safety check even though he didn't realize there was anything wrong."

"Yeah." Will nods. "It's all related somehow—but it's beyond me to figure out."

"Things work out exactly the way they're supposed to," Renee continues. "I don't think we have to know the how or the why. We just have to know it's all somehow good in the end." It occurs to me that Renee is almost answering my unasked question. I feel the burden of responsibility lift as I realize she's right. I don't have to understand, I just have to be open to the experience and see where it takes me. That's a relief. I put my arm around her shoulder, pull her close, and kiss her in the soft spot right below her ear. The smell of her perfume fills the air around her.

"What's that for?" she asks, laughing.

"For being you."

We don't stay too much longer because Will is getting tired. I doubt he'll be able to go back to school sooner than next week, boring TV or not. I promise to keep bringing his assignments over. Renee has to get home to work with some other kids on a group project, so I drive to her house.

When I pull up at the curb, I stop and turn off the car. "I want you to know that what you said at Will's, about not having to understand how it all works? And how we can be confident knowing that everything is happening the way it should? That really helped me." I brush my hand against her cheek. "I was starting to feel like I had this huge responsibility. Now I think just accepting it is enough."

"I'm glad. There will always be more of what we don't understand than what we do understand." I lean forward and gently touch my lips to hers, and she responds by kissing me harder. I put my hand on the back of her neck and pull her closer, kissing her fiercely. *I really love this girl,* I think, and it fills me with happiness. She pulls away after a few moments and says, a little breathlessly, "I'd really love to continue this, but I have to meet up with my project group. Do you want to come over after dinner to study?"

"Yes . . . to be continued?"

"We'll see," she says with a wink. I watch her walk across the lawn to the front door. Ostensibly to be sure she can get inside, but really because I just love watching her.

On the way home, I decide to go for a run. The weather is fantastic and I don't want to get out of shape now that soccer is over. Nobody's home when I get there, except the dogs, who greet me like I've been away for years. I take the stairs two at a time up to my room and change into shorts and a T-shirt and my running shoes. Ralph and Speck get excited when they see my shoes, thinking perhaps a walk might be in store for them. They run in circles around my legs, almost tripping me in their excitement.

"Sorry guys, maybe later." They look so disappointed when I leave them inside that I decide to take them out after my run as a cool down.

After stretching and some warm-ups, I start a slow jog on the road that leads out of town. Even though it's warm, the air has a bit of an edge, like the cold is just waiting to return. The earthy smell of fallen leaves and cut grass fills the air as people get home from work and take advantage of the nice weather to mow the lawn one last time. I'm feeling strong and loose, so I pick up the pace and decide to make this a long run. When I get to the outskirts of town, I turn onto the road that goes past the lagoons. The sun is dropping low on the horizon, turning the sky orange and gold. I look over at the field and the tree where Will crashed his car and see that it has a big gash in its side. But also, what I didn't notice that night in the dark, I see that it's covered in blazing red leaves. The light from the setting sun makes it seem like the tree is on fire, glowing gold around the crimson leaves. And I also see, or maybe just imagine, another light. Through the mostly bare trees it seems like there's a soft glow coming from where the stargazing rock sits on the shore of the lagoon. A feeling of incredible well-being washes over me. I don't stop to look, I just keep running. I don't need to see it to believe it's real.

I hear honking overhead and look up to see a flock of geese pass over me. They're flying in a *V*, and for a few moments, the lead goose flies directly above me, in sync with my pace. Then I reach the end of the road and turn left. The geese keep flying, heading south, and I run on, toward home.

Acknowledgments

I originally wrote *The Field* over nine years ago. Since then, I've experienced a series of tremendous changes in my life, which proved to be exceptionally challenging yet resulted in a positive transformation for me on every level. I'd like to gratefully recognize those people who were there, and continue to be there, to support, nurture, and encourage me on this journey.

My brother and sister-in-law, Rob and Liz, for saving me. My children, Alex and Katie, for loving me. My dad, Hank, his girlfriend, Joan, and my brother Mark for always listening and supporting me. The "Guru Girls"—Jennifer, Leslie, Sarah, Celia, Jenny, and Debbie—(and their spouses) for sticking with me and lifting me up. Virginia for always being there. Katy for joining me on my forward path and always being ready for an adventure. Elizabeth for taking me dancing. Susie and Susan for being true "girlfriends." Lilly for hikes and more dancing. Leslie, Kate, and Nancy for opening your homes to me. Annie's class for listening. Mary's group for supporting me. Thank you, thank you, thank you all. I wouldn't be where I am now without you. The best is yet to come.

Also, a big thank-you to Tom Reale of Brown Books Publishing for loving *The Field* and choosing to reissue it and *Indian Summer* as well as the third book, *Catalyst,* and the as yet untitled—and unwritten—fourth book in the family. Everyone at Brown Books "gets" my books and is wonderful to work with. What more could an author ask for? It's my hope that all of you "get" my books, too.

About the Author

Tracy Richardson wasn't always a writer, but she was always a reader. Her favorite book growing up was *A Wrinkle in Time* by Madeleine L'Engle. In a weird way that book has even shaped her life through odd synchronicities. She has a degree in biology like Mrs. Murry, and, without realizing it, she named her children Alex and Katie after Meg's parents.

Tracy uses her science background in her writing through her emphasis on environmental issues, metaphysics, and science fiction. When she's not writing, you'll find her doing any number of creative activities—painting furniture, knitting sweaters, or cooking something. She lives in Indianapolis, and, in case you're wondering, yes, she's been to the Indianapolis 500.